# SECRETS

# BEGIN

SECRETS
BEGIN

# SECRETS BEGIN

## Ronald Hale

**SITE PUBLISHING**
7330 Staples Mill Road #106
Richmond, VA 23228
sitepublishingtoday@gmail.com

Cover design: Jen Ciner @ JenC Designs

Printed in the United States of America

First Edition: January 2022
10  9  8  7  6  5  4  3  2  1

ISBN: 978-0-9796241-8-6
Library of Congress Control Number: 2021912385

**Author's Contact Information**
Ronald Hale
email: secretsbegin2022@gmail.com

But I tell you, *love* your enemies and *pray* for those who persecute you...

Matthew 5:44

# Secrets Begin

Book 2 of the SECRETS Trilogy

# CHAPTER 1

**It was the first day of school,** and I was more excited than a pig at mealtime. I'd been double promoted from the fourth grade straight into the sixth, and that made me the youngest sixth grader in school. It was definitive proof that I was smarter than all of them, and I was proud as punch. I grinned as I stepped out the door, already envisioning what it would be like to wield my intellectual superiority over my classmates.

With a spring in my step, I headed down the block, squinting against the bright sun. Two short miles later, I stood in front of my new school, James P. Timothy Middle

School, buried in the heart of Boston. I paused at the door, my grin unwavering. I took a deep breath and crossed the threshold with my shoulders held high. I was confident my first day as the smartest sixth grader in school was going to be remarkable.

I'd even taken extra care with my outfit so my new classmates would know I was not only book smart, but fashionable, too. They'd see I was one of the cool kids. I didn't have many options to help me dress the part, but I'd donned my Salvation Army best: a pair of dark brown, corduroy pants and a light blue Oxford shirt. The shirt had a noticeable bleach stain on the left collar, but no one would care, I reasoned, bending over to lace up my brand-new, black, shell-toe, Adidas sneakers. They were my most prized possession; walking in them, I stood tall and forgot the sorry state of the rest of my hand-me-down clothes.

As I made a left through the doors and strutted down a graffiti-covered hallway, I looked over the crowd of kids leaning up against lockers and walls. Faces of every color stared back at me. I waved and smiled at everyone whose eyes caught mine, and even spotted a few cute girls checking me out. Just then, I overheard two hecklers poking fun at my clothes. Lifting my chin, I kept moving, pretending I hadn't heard. My confidence wavered. Feeling suddenly self-conscious, I noticed that the farther down the hall I walked, the more eyes followed me, and not out of admiration. I was the butt of their collective joke, even though not one person had said anything to me directly.

Every kid in the hall was wearing brand-new, name-brand clothing, and all from the most recent collections. My best Salvation Army clothes looked like rags next to their outfits. My heart pounded in my ears, drowning out the hum of conversations and laughter. It suddenly came crashing down that I was not only the youngest kid in school. I was also the only one poor enough to wear hand-me-downs. Suddenly, being the smartest didn't matter.

For a moment, I thought about running, but my legs turned to jelly. Trying not to look desperate, I stole a glance down at my outfit, willing it to look cool enough to fit in. But even my shell-toe Adidas sneakers didn't make me feel better. I'd overheard another kid whispering to his friend that they were out of style.

I headed toward the restroom, forcing my way through the crowd of onlookers. Retreating inside, I stared at my reflection in the bathroom mirror. My embarrassment was written all over my face. My anger spiked. How could my mother have sent me to school in hand-me-downs? Didn't she realize I would be the laughingstock of the entire school? I turned on the faucet to splash water on my face, trying to cool down. I sucked in a deep breath and held it for a moment. My shoulders sagged as I let out a heavy breath, dropping my chin. I wondered how I would make it through the rest of the day without being the butt of every joke. Glancing at my reflection once more, I shook my head, trying to muster my courage.

As I turned away from the mirror, a flash of white caught my eye. Looking for the source, I spotted an obvious rip down the left side of my pants, revealing my underwear. My heart jumped up into my throat, and I let out an involuntary screech before managing to swallow it back down. This couldn't be happening. But it was. Now my outfit practically *screamed* "poor." What was I going to do? Urgently, I wrestled with the tear, trying to conceal it. But the more I tried to fix it, the worse it got.

Tears welled up in my eyes, but I quickly brushed them away. The last thing I needed was for someone to walk into the bathroom and see me crying. That would just make everything worse.

Finally, I gave up on the rip. It was useless. I was about to become the joke of the entire sixth grade. I'd be stuck with their mockery for the next nine months, and there was nothing I could do about it. *Why do I have to be so poor?* As the thought echoed through my mind, a deep and fiery rage rose up within me. *It's not fair!*

Somehow, my anger fueled me to face my demons head-on. I kicked open the restroom door. Head held high, I walked out... and straight into Colin Smith.

Everyone knew Colin. Even in grade school, he'd been the kid to avoid. Short, fat, and with a hairline starting at his eyebrows, Colin was notorious for doing what most bullies do: taking kids' lunch money, picking on nerds, and scaring the weak and defenseless.

I couldn't help but notice that just like the other kids in school, Colin was dressed to impress. With his navy-blue Nike sweatsuit and brand-new pair of all-white, Nike Air Force Ones, he looked like a poster boy for Nike. Even his canvas bookbag rocked the Nike swoosh. Taking in his ensemble, I felt envy well up inside, mixing with my rage.

Normally I'd have steered clear of him, but today, I'd already had enough. I was too angry to care who was in my way. As I rolled up on Colin, my hands were already balled into fists at my sides.

"Khalil Gilliam," he sneered, his eyes roving over my outfit. "What are you up to?"

"On my way to homeroom." I leaned in, daring him to say something smart.

Colin's eyes made their way down to my bookbag, and his stare drew my own. Oh no. To my dismay, I noticed the seams had started to pull apart and unravel almost all the way around the bag. I groaned inwardly. Could nothing I owned be good enough? My angry confidence slipped, and I looked away, trying to hide the embarrassment I was sure was all over my face again.

My mind raced as I wondered what Colin would do next. The glory I'd felt that morning at my double promotion had completely vanished. The only thing that was real now was my imminent humiliation. What would

Colin do in response to my shabbiness? Would he put me on display in front of the others? Colin was well-known for a reason, so I expected the worst. My heart pounded violently, and I felt my breathing speed up as I waited for him to expose me. *Is it too late to transfer to a new school?* I wondered desperately.

I held my breath, but nothing happened. Finally, I looked up. Colin hadn't moved or even reacted. I couldn't read his face. What was his deal? His bullying usually took a fraction of a second to happen. Maybe I was too shabby to be bullied. Was that even a thing? I couldn't just stand there forever, though, so to avoid further embarrassment, I cautiously stepped past him, letting out a silent sigh of relief as I pulled away and out of his sight.

Unfortunately, as I made my way towards homeroom, I spotted Zoe Turner heading in my direction with a group of girls following closely behind her. With her curly, black, shoulder-length hair, and smooth, sepia complexion, there was no doubt Zoe was the prettiest girl in school. Her looks and her ballerina-like figure turned heads wherever she went, and she knew it. I'd noticed her the year before, but she was two years older and way out of my league, so mostly I'd just admired her from afar - making sure never to get caught staring, of course. Everyone knew better than to risk her wrath.

In addition to her stunning looks, Zoe's fashion style was the envy of many. Rumored to be the daughter of a successful Boston attorney, she wore clothes that highlighted both her exquisite fashion sense and her daddy's money.

Gorgeous as she was, her attitude was the opposite. Zoe was the mean girl to the mean girls, and everyone else, too. She was known for verbally attacking anyone she thought was beneath her, which was pretty much everyone, especially poor and darker-skinned kids. I fell into both categories.

As she drew near, I moved closer to the wall and took a deep breath. Mentally, I tried to will myself into invisibility. But my habit of watching her sashay down the halls did me in, and my not-invisible eyes rose up and met hers.

We were still fifty feet apart when she spoke. "Hey, Black Boy," she spat in my direction, her voice dripping with condescension. Some of her faithful kiss-butt followers sneered; others burst into laughter.

I tried not to show it, but I was shocked. No one outside of my family had ever called me by that name. It was awful when my family did it, but hearing Zoe mock me for the color of my skin was so much worse. Volatile as my emotions had already been that day, my first impulse was to punch her in the face. But I steeled myself and, instead of reacting to her name-calling, looked away and continued walking.

Unwilling to let it go, she called out even louder, "Dag, boy, you're blacker than midnight. You better stay out of the sun, Tar Baby!"

I was even closer than before, so the extra volume was just for show. It worked. More students laughed this time, and her girls were practically bowled over, holding onto one another. All the laughter seemed to spur Zoe on; her taunts became even meaner. "I hope the lights don't go off in class today. The teacher might mark you absent, you black fool."

Her jeers rang in my ears and my classmates' laughter filled the hallway as I finally drew even with her.

Amazingly, I'd managed to keep my cool thus far. Trying to take the higher ground, I held my head as high as I could and just glared at her as I walked by.

"What are you staring at, Blackie?" she snarled in return.

At the addition of yet another slur against me, my last modicum of patience melted away. I'd already passed her, so I spun on my heel, ready to let her have it. But she'd turned away, still cackling with her girls. I sent daggers towards them all with my eyes, then turned again only to realize I'd made it to the end of the hallway and was now standing directly in front of my homeroom class. I took a deep breath and slowly let it out, turning to enter the classroom.

I'd no more than walked through the door when I spotted Elijah Rogers, yet another school bully I'd been hoping to avoid. Grinning as he spotted me, he stuck up his middle finger. I groaned to myself. *Could this day get any worse?* It had already been such a far cry from what I'd imagined that I wasn't sure how much more I could take.

Elijah was a fairly good-looking kid except for

his pole-like frame and the smug grin on his face. The expression he wore told me Zoe's wisecracks were just the beginning of what I had coming my way. As I looked over at him warily, I noticed he was wearing a pair of dingy, old, high-water, blue jeans and a wrinkled, yellow, Polo shirt that didn't appear to fit him quite right. In an instant, I realized what seemed off: I wasn't the only poor kid in school. Elijah was poor, too. Unfortunately for me, I knew Elijah tried to make himself look good by making other kids look bad.

"Watch out, everybody. Doctor Midnight is in the house." He let out a roar of laughter as I walked by.

I leveled him my best fighting stare and made my way to an open desk at the back of the classroom. As soon as I raised my eyes again, he pinned me with a stare in return and said loudly, "Has anybody ever told you that you look like Kunta Kinte from the movie *Roots*?"

My jaw dropped, completely shocked he'd gone there. Immediately, the room exploded into laughter. Some people were laughing so hard I could actually see tears, and a couple of others fell out of their chairs, cracking up.

Growing up in the hood, there were only really two big no-nos: Never talk about a person's mother - that alone would get you punched in the face every single time - and never call a kid "Kunta Kinte." It was practically like saying someone was a slave. Had he called me any other name, I'd have ignored him. But I couldn't let "Kunta Kinte" slide.

I figured there was no way this day could deteriorate further, but I'd be damned if I was going to let this be how I went down. Watching them all laugh at my expense, the rage that had been burning inside me all morning finally boiled over. I was going to make sure I never had another day like this, and to do that, I needed to put Elijah in check.

I slammed my fists on my desk, heaved myself out of my seat and, veins popping in my forehead, made my way straight to him. I was determined to knock a few teeth down his throat.

"You think that's funny, Elijah, you punk?" My raised fist had a clear line of impact with his jaw. Before I could unleash a left hook to the bottom of his chin, though, Elijah stood up. His eyes weren't on me. They were focused on the front of the class where our teacher, Mr. Poindexter, had been standing watching the exchange.

"Get back to your seat, Mr. Gilliam," he said with a scowl.

It was only my first day, but I'd heard Mr. Poindexter was a former drill sergeant turned art teacher. Ready as I was to take out Elijah, I wasn't willing to go head-to-head with an adult with that background, at least not on day one. Giving Elijah one more venomous stare, I withdrew my proposed assault and headed back to my seat.

As I stomped down the aisle between the desks, Elijah dealt yet another emotional blow. Pointing at me, he shouted, "Look at that hole in his pants!" The once-small rip near my hip had grown again and now had me exposed, revealing my dingy, white Fruit of the Looms underneath.

I knew I couldn't react, not after just being reprimanded by Mr. Poindexter. I clenched my fists and ground my teeth to keep from exploding, but inside, I was seething. Elijah was going to pay for his comments, as were the rest of my classmates for their smug amusement. I found my seat at the back of the room, threw myself into the chair, crossed my arms on my desk and laid my head on them, trying not to listen to Elijah leading the class in a loud chant of, "Poor Black Boy, Poor Black Boy!"

*Would it never stop?* After several rounds, I lifted my head, shooting an accusatory glance at Mr. Poindexter. He'd put on such an authoritarian show moments earlier. Where was he now? Why was he allowing me to take all this abuse, and on my first day? Was he deaf to their name-calling? I stared at him, willing him to look at me until he raised his gaze and met my eyes. But I saw no help there, just a blank, detached look. His silence was a clear indicator that my teachers cared as little for me as my peers. With this realization, the tiny spark of hope I hadn't realized I still held in my heart went dark and cold.

Feeling helpless, I shot Elijah another hard stare, but it was pointless. He was unfazed. I closed my eyes and dropped my head again, waiting for the bell to end my homeroom horror.

When the bell rang, I trudged into the bathroom once more for a momentary reprieve from my classmates' cruelty and another attempt at concealing the rip in my pants. There was really no fixing it. I stood motionless in front of the mirror, reliving Zoe's and Elijah's taunts. I hated being different, but they were right. My skin was really dark, a lot blacker than any of the other kids in school.

For the rest of the day, I endured being called Tar Baby, Doctor Midnight, Blackie, Black Boy, Ink Spot, Nigga Baby, stupid, ugly, stinky, and every other degrading name my schoolmates could concoct. The name-calling was awful, but it was their incessant laughter that hurt the worst.

By the time the final class bell rang, I felt completely broken. I headed glumly back to homeroom, my shoulders hunched in defeat, knowing I still had more viciousness headed my way from Elijah and the others. This time, though, I didn't bother considering going postal on them. I took my seat at the back of the class, braced myself for their abuse, and stared at the clock on the wall. It wouldn't be long before the first day of school was over, and the verbal and emotional attacks would finally end. At least until tomorrow.

When the bell sounded, I flung my bookbag over my shoulder and quickly headed for the door. Before I could make it, though, Mr. Poindexter grabbed me by the back of the arm.

"Don't worry about it, Gilliam. Kids can be cruel. Just keep your head up. It'll get better," he offered.

I offered him a tight smile and shrugged out of his grasp. His words gave me no comfort. He had already shown me he didn't really care.

I headed out the exit and down the steps, thoroughly beat from the cruel day. Dragging my heels, I made my way home. I couldn't believe I'd started my first day of sixth grade so elated only to have it end like this.

# CHAPTER 2

**Walking in the door,** I made a beeline for the bedroom I shared with my brothers, Damien and Stephon. Throwing myself on my bed, I stared up at the ceiling. *Why does my skin have to be so much darker than everyone else's?* I thought angrily. I was noticeably darker than everyone I knew, even my siblings. It was a constant source of ridicule, and I hated it. The toughest part was that my sixth-grade year had just started. *How am I possibly going to make it through?* I felt helpless. The darkness began to close in. But before it took me over completely, an idea popped into my head.

Jumping off the bed, I dashed out of my bedroom to the family bathroom and turned on the bathtub faucet. I tapped my heel impatiently, waiting for the water to warm, then twisted the stopper closed to fill the bathtub with hot water.

"This should work," I stated aloud. "I'll no longer be 'Black Boy.'"

Peeking out the bathroom door, I could see Dakota and Michelle doing their homework in the living room. I knew Stephon and Damien were outdoors shooting hoops. The coast was clear. I dashed to the laundry room, and there it was, sitting right on the shelf above the washer: Mom's big bottle of Clorox bleach. I grabbed it and rushed back to the bathroom, nearly tripping over my feet in my excitement. Locking the door behind me, I unscrewed the cap, then turned the bottle completely upside down and poured half the contents into the hot water, a huge grin spreading across my face. I had no idea exactly how it would work, but I was confident I was about to be a different person. Whatever side effects I had to endure would be worth it.

Screwing the bleach cap back on, I set the bottle on the edge of the sink and took one last look into the mirror at my black skin. In a few minutes, my life would be better. I quickly undressed and lowered my 10-year-old frame into the hot, smelly water. I lay still and waited. In just a few minutes, my skin began to itch like crazy. I figured that meant the bleach was working. I reminded myself this was simply the cost. I took a deep breath - a mistake, as the whole room smelled strongly of bleach - and tried to focus on the endgame: lighter skin. I was committed to sticking it out.

Despite my resolve, my efforts were short-lived. The itch soon became unbearable. Seeking relief, I began to scrub my body violently for a few minutes. When I could not take the itch and smell anymore, I pulled the stopper and drained the tub. I was still itching, so I took a quick shower and scrubbed myself with soap and shampoo, hoping to calm the itch but also get rid of the smell of bleach. Turning off the water, I reached for my towel but only found Mom's. The rest of the towels were in the closet down the hall, so I grabbed it. I overheard Stephon and Damien in the hallway; they were back. It was time to see how light-skinned I'd become. I quickly dried off, then gingerly stepped in front of the bathroom mirror again. Ready to see the new me, I wiped away the fog and stared at my reflection. My eyes, bright and hopeful, stared back at me from a face as black as ever. Quickly, I scanned the rest of my body. No change at all. What had I done wrong? I'd gotten nowhere, and my skin still stung and burned. I could feel the wail rising from my chest up into my throat and struggled to hold it in. Warm tears spilled out over my cheeks. Had I taken a Clorox bath for nothing? If Mom found out about the wasted bleach, I was dead.

"Hurry up out of the bathroom, Black Boy!" Stephon banged on the bathroom door, making me jump.

"I'll be right out," I said as gruffly as I could, wiping away the tears. I quickly tucked the bottle of bleach into the cabinet under the sink to retrieve later.

As I unlocked the bathroom door, Stephon came flying in with his fist raised. He connected with my chest, knocking me backwards into the tub.

"That's for making me wait." He stood over me,

grinning. "The next time you hear me knocking, you open the door, you black punk." He sniffed the air, looking around. "What were you doing in here? It smells like bleach."

Pushing myself up out of the tub, I said nothing and stepped around him to the door. As I walked out of the bathroom, Damien, Michelle, and Dakota all giggled at me. They'd seen Stephon's abuse go down, but none of them asked if I was okay. Shooting them all a glare, I rubbed my chest where he'd punched me, hoping the pain there would settle, and headed back to my room.

# CHAPTER 3

**By the time my eyes** popped open the next morning, I had decided there was no way I was repeating the previous day. The next person who made fun of me was getting knocked out, no matter who they were.

As I approached the school, I noticed a group of kids from my homeroom class laughing as they sneaked glances over their shoulders at me.

"What's up, Black Boy?" one of them shouted in my direction, encouraging the others.

Lengthening my stride, I reached him in under two seconds. Without preamble, I pulled back my fist and punched him square in the mouth. Not waiting for him to hit back, I slammed him onto the asphalt, continuing my assault with a few more well-placed thumps.

Glancing up, I noticed the kids outside the school had clustered around us, watching the scene unfold. Before things could get too crazy, though, a hush fell over the crowd. I paused, my fist raised, and looked up. Mr. Poindexter was bearing down on us. Before I could react, he had us both by the collar and was escorting us straight to the principal's office.

"Call these boys' parents immediately, please," he instructed the principal's assistant. She nodded and picked up the phone.

Not good! I knew Mom worked just around the corner from the school. But I didn't have a chance to worry about it because Mr. Poindexter still had me by the collar and was pushing me through the principal's door.

Principal Elder looked up and raised his eyebrows as the three of us entered his office.

"What happened?" he questioned.

Pushing us down into two hard, plastic chairs near the door, Mr. Poindexter approached him and, leaning down low, began whispering in Principal Elder's ear. Occasionally, his eyes cut over in our direction. *What is he saying about me?* I crossed my arms over my chest, ready to defend myself again. But the pressure got to my classmate first.

"He attacked me for no reason!" my classmate rang out. "I was hanging out with some other kids from our homeroom class when out of nowhere he just started hitting me." His voice trembled with fear.

I couldn't believe it. Was he really trying to pin this on me after all the abuse I'd taken from them yesterday?

"You lying, no-good, mother…" I leaped out of my chair and spun to face him, ready for round two.

"Sit down, Mr. Gilliam," Mr. Poindexter demanded. He strode back towards us, grabbed my shoulder, and pushed me back down into the chair. "This is neither the time nor the place for your disrespectful behavior." I shot my classmate an angry glare.

"That's right, son," Principal Elder chimed in. "You're in enough trouble as it is." Reaching into his desk drawer, he pulled out an ancient, tattered book. He flipped through for a moment, then launched into a long, boring speech about what the student handbook deemed "appropriate conduct on school premises."

I'd mostly zoned out by the time the principal's assistant walked into the office. But fear shot through me when I saw Mom enter the office right behind her. I knew Mom worked two jobs, sometimes three, just to support our family. The last thing she needed was to lose pay because I couldn't control myself.

"Ms. Gilliam has arrived," she announced, then left the room, closing the door behind her.

I risked a glance at Mom's face and immediately regretted it. She was clearly fuming.

"I'm sorry we had to call you at work, Ms. Gilliam," Principal Elder said, "but we had no other choice."

"What did he do this time?" she asked, rolling up her sleeves. I knew what that meant. I needed to get out of there, fast. But there was nowhere to go.

"Why don't you tell your mother what you did?"

I looked at Principal Elder, then at Mom, and then back at the principal. I sat frozen as Mom stopped in front of me, my mouth glued shut. Slowly, she traced the side of my face with her fingers.

*Maybe she's not so upset after all,* I thought briefly, a sliver of hope welling inside. A half-second later, though, I realized how wrong I was. The back of her hand connected with my face, hard enough to make my ears ring.

"What did you do, child?" she demanded.

I was too afraid to tell her I'd been in a fight. She'd beat me to a pulp for sure. But I had to say something, had to defend my honor. Taking a deep breath, I stood up and said loudly, "He started it!"

"Boy, do you want me to whip your narrow ass in this office?" Mom demanded.

That had me back in my seat with my mouth shut. My anger boiled over once again. *It's all her fault anyway,* I told myself as I folded my arms across my chest. She was the one who had sent me to school in hand-me-downs in the first place. All of this could have been avoided if I'd had new clothes like everyone else.

I'd told myself I wasn't saying anything more, but Mom's stare was unrelenting. Caving under the pressure, I finally let it all spill out. "I punched him in the mouth for calling me 'Black Boy.'"

"You did *what*? And you did it *why*?" She stepped closer to me, her fists balled. Anytime Mom asked two questions consecutively, it was a sure-fire sign you were in for a thumping. This time, it looked like it was going down right in the principal's office.

Without warning, Mom grabbed me by the back of the arm, dragged me over to the fancy chair near the principal's desk, and threw me over the arm. Then she pulled out the belt she always carried in her purse just for occasions like this, she told us once, where her kids stepped out of line.

Knowing what was coming, I tried to escape. I couldn't help it. I leapt out from under her raised arm and dashed around the principal's desk, scattering papers everywhere before skidding into the bookshelf against the far wall, knocking off several books and a large potted plant. Mom was right behind me. Trying to stay ahead, I circled the desk like a maniac, round and round. But she was relentless. I needed a way out. Spotting my exit, I headed for the office door, about to make my break. But Mom caught me. Hauling me back over to the fancy chair, she threw me over the arm once again. This time, before I could escape again, she began thrashing my backside, covering everything from my shoulders down to the backs of my legs. In the background, I could hear my classmate cheering Mom on.

"Whip his ass, Ms. Gilliam," he shouted, bursting with excitement. "Tear him a new one!"

"Help me," I pleaded. But Principal Elder and Mr. Poindexter simply stood by and watched, smirking. Just when I was wondering whether someone ought to call the police and report child abuse, the thrashing finally came to an end. Apparently, Mom was all tuckered out because she leaned on the matching fancy chair and breathed heavily.

"Now, apologize," she demanded huffily.

There was no way I was signing up for another round of beating, so I quickly, albeit resentfully, apologized to Principal Elder, Mr. Poindexter, and my classmate for my behavior. They sent me home for the day, supposedly to prevent any further fights. But I knew that wouldn't be the case.

When Mom arrived home later that day, she beat me again. This time, she told me it was not because I'd beat up the kid who'd called me names. This thrashing was for running around like a fool in the principal's office. She said I should have known better than to embarrass her in public.

In addition, she sent me to bed without dinner. My growling stomach, coupled with the anger I felt at the injustice of it all, kept me up well into the night. I was still awake when Mom padded into my room, believing me to be fast asleep, and whispered in my ear, "Next time, you better knock his teeth out." Noticing my eyes fly open at her statement, she smiled at me lovingly, kissed me on the forehead, and headed out of the room.

I stared at her retreating back. Was she crazy? If it was okay for me to defend myself, then why did I get my butt whipped, and twice at that? I didn't understand.

I was back to fighting the next day. This time, Principal Elder decided not to call my mother. After the show she'd put on in his office, I figured he thought she might kill me if she found out I was causing trouble again.

Instead, he chastised me sternly about my behavior. I nodded dutifully, and he sent me back to class. The next day, I fought again, and he rebuked me again. Soon we were repeating the charade almost daily. But with no real consequences, it was easy to ignore his lecturing.

It didn't take long for word to get around that I was not the same scrawny, doubly-promoted kid who staggered into school on the first day. I was now a ten-year-old pain in the neck, and everybody knew better than to mess with me.

News about my fists spread fast. Some called me "Floyd Mayweather," and others called me "One-Punch Gilliam." I quickly became one of the most feared kids at school. I was thrilled the name-calling had stopped. But what had happened to me on the first day of school still stuck with me.

Before my promotion into the sixth grade, I'd been an excellent student. But since starting middle school, I'd dropped from getting almost straight A's to bringing home a solid row of C's on my report card. Curiously, no one seemed to notice or care. To my siblings, I looked the same;

they didn't see I'd had to become a fighter to survive. Mom was the only one who knew I'd been ridiculed at school, and I was too afraid to talk with her or my brothers or sisters about the change that was happening to me. What if they didn't understand? Or worse, if they blamed me for the whole scenario? After all, my siblings had made fun of me the same way my classmates had.

So I kept quiet at home, and as long as I did, no one seemed to notice the changes in me. It was like I had become invisible to them.

# CHAPTER 4

**It was a perfect fall day,** and everyone was hanging out in the school courtyard, including the middle school teachers. I was my new, fighting self, complete with the hefty chip on my shoulder. Looking for a reason to knock someone out, I noticed Colin and a few other tough kids standing in front of the local convenience store just down the street from the school. They were talking to each other but staring in my direction. Without fear, I strolled over to them and grinned, feeling good just knowing I could. No longer was I terrified. Now, *I* was the terrifying one.

"What's up, Colin?" I said, making the peace sign.

He just ignored me and turned away.

"Yo, Colin, you don't hear me talking to you?" I stood in front of him, nose to nose, but he still didn't respond.

Smiling smugly at his obvious fear, I headed toward the entrance of the school, chuckling to myself.

"Fat boy is tripping!" I grinned, sauntering to my locker to grab my books for first-period class. As I turned around, I discovered Elijah right behind me, clearly out of breath. He'd been trying to get on my good side since I'd taken out that kid on the second day of school.

"What's up, jokester?" I spoke.

"You haven't heard?" he panted.

"Heard what?" I replied dryly, slamming shut my locker door.

"Colin and his boys said they are going to beat you up after school today."

"What?" I stiffened briefly but quickly regained my composure. Taking a breath, I continued more casually. "When did you hear this?"

"When you left the convenience store, Jon Butler told

Colin that the entire sixth-grade class thinks you are the best fighter in school."

I rolled my eyes. Jon Butler, a tall, slender mulatto kid from the suburbs, was always a meddler.

"So what?" I laughed as we proceeded towards homeroom. "I'm not afraid of Colin and those punks, man."

"That's not all of it," he continued, looking serious. His breathing was almost back to normal now. "Jon also told Colin you said you could beat him in a one-on-one fight."

"Stop with all this gossip," I waved a hand in his direction. "Everyone knows Jon is a liar. I don't have time to entertain his foolery."

"Well, that's the rumor going around."

"The next time you want to pass a rumor concerning me," I glared at him, "don't!"

"I just thought you should know, Khalil," he shrugged, clapping me on the back. "That's what friends are for, right?"

"Friends?" I jeered. "If you don't get out of my face..." My eyes locked in on his jaw. I thought about taking him out, but maybe, just maybe, the rumor about Colin wanting to fight me was true, so I held off.

As Elijah and I took our seats in the back of the classroom, Colin and three guys walked in and approached me.

"We need to talk, Khalil," Colin announced, loud enough for the whole class to hear. I glanced towards the door. Mr. Poindexter was still out in the hallway, chatting with another teacher.

I stood. "What's up, Colin?" I asked, my fists clenched, ready for any sudden movement.

"You're getting your butt whipped after school today," he asserted.

Just then, Mr. Poindexter stepped back inside the room. Colin lowered his voice.

"Jon told me you said you could drop me if we fought one-on-one."

"Whatever. Stop playing, Colin," I nudged him hard on the shoulder, but he shoved me back.

"We'll see who's playing when school is over, you punk!" he hissed before turning and walking away, his boys trailing in his wake. It looked like whatever he had planned was going down whether I liked it or not.

News of the imminent fight spread quickly. By the time the final bell rang, students were gathered in groups

35

outside the school entrance, making bets on the fight. No one seemed to know who the winner would be. Half of the school had money on me, and the other half was betting on Colin.

I grabbed my bookbag out of my locker and walked toward what I figured would either be a decisive victory or my ultimate humiliation. I was going to do everything I could to make sure it was the first. I stepped out of the building and took a cursory look around. Colin and his boys were visibly absent, but onlookers surrounded the school entrance. I decided to take this chance to show everyone how tough I was. I tossed my bookbag to the ground, took off my shirt, revealing my tiny muscular frame, and pranced around the entrance to the school grounds.

"You scared, man?" Elijah questioned quietly, approaching me from the side.

"Do I look scared?" I said angrily, mostly for show.

"A little bit," he shot back. "If I were you, I would be peeing my pants."

"That's why you are not me," I said dismissively.

"Yep, and today I don't want to be you, either."

"Are they here yet?" I shouted, hoping everyone could see how tough I was. "I've been waiting to beat Colin and his punk boys all day. Where are they?" I practically screamed.

As I shadowboxed the air, out of the corner of my eye I spotted Zoe approaching me. To my surprise, she walked up to me, put her hand on my shoulder, and said encouragingly, "You can take him, Khalil. I believe in you." She gave a slight squeeze before letting go and walking away.

"Thanks!" I replied, feeling a little bemused as I watched her walk away. It was the first time Zoe had ever said anything nice to me, and though I wasn't sure why her attitude had changed, I realized the stakes had just increased. No matter how scared I was, I couldn't lose, not after Zoe's vote of confidence.

The tension in the air was palpable as the minutes dragged on. Still, Colin and his boys were nowhere to be found. The agonizing silence allowed plenty of time for my thoughts to plague me. What if I lost? What would Zoe and the rest of the sixth-grade class think then? I'd lose all the credibility I'd built over the past few months. I paced around the schoolyard, hoping no one would notice my increasing angst. Mostly however, I hoped Colin and his boys wouldn't show. That would make it an easy win for me.

Twenty minutes after the final bell, I began to tire of waiting for Colin and his buddies. *Where are they? Are they going to back out? Maybe they are afraid. Perhaps Colin and his boys realized that they are no match for me after all. Maybe I am the best fighter in the sixth grade.*

This thought gave me a fresh wave of confidence; I relaxed a bit. Soon, I began joking with the other kids, considering myself victorious already.

After another ten minutes, most kids seemed to have given up on the fight and began to disperse. Heaving a silent sigh of relief, I allowed myself to bask in the newfound respect I felt I'd just earned from the school.

With nearly everyone gone, I decided I might as well make my way home. I pulled my shirt back on, threw my bookbag over my right shoulder and began the short walk home.

Just a few moments later, I heard laughter and shouts behind me. I recognized Colin's voice among them. Without even looking back, I fled. Given I was already about forty or so yards ahead of them, I easily put enough distance between me and them to make it home safely, though I arrived entirely out of breath.

I headed for my room, slamming the door behind me, and fell face down on my bed. Turning my head just enough to breathe, I stared dejectedly towards the window. I dodged a bullet and managed to not get myself cornered, outnumbered, or embarrassed today, but Colin lived right around the corner from us. I couldn't avoid him forever.

Just then, my brother, Stephon, walked into the room with a bologna and cheese sandwich and a glass of milk.

"What are you looking at?" he asked, taking a big bite out of his sandwich, and pinning me with his sharp stare.

"Nothing," I said, rolling onto my back and averting my gaze towards the ceiling. "Just don't feel like going out today."

Stephon took another bite out of his sandwich and gulped down some milk, his stare unwavering.

"You're lying." He finished the sandwich in two more bites, then grabbed me by the collar. "I can see it in your eyes. Now, tell me the truth before I hurt you."

"Okay, okay!" I relented. "Colin and some other kids from school tried to jump me today."

"Colin?" He loosened his grip. "Fat Colin from around the corner? He tried to jump you?"

"Yeah."

"I'll be right back." He walked out of the room. Ten minutes later he was back, another sandwich and glass of milk in hand. "You can go outside now."

"But what if they are out there, waiting for me?" I knew I sounded like a scared little punk, which was the last thing I wanted my older brother to think. But I was scared.

"I'm not going to tell you again." He set down his glass and balled up his fist. His eyes zeroed in on my chin. "Take your black butt outside, now."

Cautiously, I peeked my head out the front door. Outside, a few kids in the park across the street were playing kickball. They beckoned to me, and I carefully approached, keeping my eyes peeled. The game resumed.

Just as I started to relax, I saw Colin and two of his boys heading my way from across the field. I froze mid-play as they got closer. There was no out for me now.

"What's up, Khalil?" Colin called out.

I stood tall as they approached, aiming for a show of bravado.

"We were joking with you at school today," Colin laughed, reaching out to jab me lightly in the arm. "I didn't know you could run that fast." He grinned, and his boys echoed his laughter.

"It was a joke?" I repeated dubiously, feeling anger rise in my throat.

"Yeah, you didn't think we were serious, did you?" He rolled his eyes and laughed again. He turned to leave, still snickering to his boys as they walked away.

"I didn't think it was funny!" I shouted angrily at their retreating backs.

"You are funny, Khalil," Colin called back over his shoulder.

I watched their retreating backs until they turned the corner, wondering if Colin would tell everyone at school that my brother had fought my battle for me.

# CHAPTER 5

**The next morning,** Colin and his boys were standing in front of the local convenience store when I stopped by to pick up some early morning snacks. I took a deep breath, plastered a confident look on my face, and stepped boldly up to him.

"What's up, Khalil?" He frowned as I approached.

I stuck my chest out. "I'm chilling. What's up with you?" I was ready to fight if it came to it.

"We're chilling, too. Right, guys?"

"Yeah, we're chilling," they repeated in unison.

My confrontation seemed to be getting me nowhere, so I glared at the four of them angrily, then turned and headed into the convenience store. Scooping up my favorite snacks, I headed for the checkout line. As I stood there waiting, I overheard Jon, standing outside the door, loudly telling everyone I was all talk.

"He'll never actually take Colin on. And besides, if he does, there's no way his scrawny ass could knock him out."

With my reputation on the line, I dropped my candy on the counter and stomped out of the convenience store to challenge him.

"What did you say, you punk?" my voice rang out.

Jon spun around so fast he nearly tripped over his feet. "I... I... I didn't say anything." He looked nervously to the others for support, but none of them said a word.

Not one of them wanted to face me. Even I could feel my rage emanating off me in waves.

"That's what I thought." Pausing to shoot each of my schoolmates a hate-filled glare, I pushed roughly past Jon and headed for school, snacks forgotten.

The rush of adrenaline left my heart slamming against my ribcage for the rest of my walk. I was grateful I'd managed to save my reputation, and powerfully, too. If the looks on their faces were any indication, I was pretty sure Colin and his boys would never challenge me again. My "fight first, ask questions never" approach had left its mark.

# CHAPTER 6

**Unfortunately, even though** I'd put Colin and his followers in their place, there were plenty of other kids at school whose mockery and bullying comments proved they still deserved a beat-down. At first, the confrontations were just to protect myself and my reputation, but over the next few years, it became a pattern. I ended up in one fight after another. Mom tried yelling, beating me, and withholding dinner, but I was dead set on being who I was. Nothing she could do would change me.

A month before my eighth grade graduation, Principal Elder scheduled an emergency meeting with

Mom. He was worried that my continued reckless behavior and bad grades would transfer over to high school. He warned Mom that if I didn't straighten up quickly, the only future that awaited me was prison or an early death.

His words fell on deaf ears. "I appreciate your concern Principal Elder." Mom looked down at her wristwatch and frowned. "I'm a single mother doing my best to raise five children. Fortunately for you, in another month, Khalil will no longer be your problem. Have a good day." With that, she stood and walked out, the meeting clearly over.

Graduation came and went, and I spent the hot days of summer enjoying my freedom and trying not to worry too much about heading into high school. The day before my thirteenth birthday, about a month before I was due to enter my freshman year, I was lounging in my bedroom when Mom called me out into the living room. As I sauntered down the hall, I noticed all my siblings also sitting in the room with her, clearly waiting for me. I tensed up. I knew what this was; it had happened several times before. Mom and my brothers and sisters were about to host yet another "family intervention," and as usual, I was the guest of honor.

I approached slowly, dreading what was coming. These things were never fun, but somehow this one felt like it was going to be worse than the ones before. Mom had tears in her eyes, and everyone's faces were grim.

I stopped at the end of the hall, staring into the room. "What's going on?" I asked, looking at each of them in turn. No one said a word.

"Are you hungry?" Mom asked.

"No, I'm not. And I know you didn't call me in here just to ask that. Just tell me what's going on." Just then, there was a knock at the door.

Damien was closest; he rose to his feet, walked to the door, and twisted the knob. With a louder squeak than usual, the door swung open. To my surprise, a hefty Boston police officer and a well-dressed white woman with short blonde hair stood on the other side.

"What's this?" I shot a demanding look at my family. "Why are the police here?"

No one answered. Mom tapped her foot under the

coffee table, nervously rubbing the top of her legs with her palms.

"I'll be right back," Damien brushed past me, heading towards the bedroom at the back of the hall. Still, no one spoke. I pressed my lips together, determined to wait it out until someone gave me some answers.

In no time, Damien returned with a mangy, old suitcase in his hand. He thrust it towards me, but I stepped back, refusing to take it. He shrugged and dropped it on the floor by my feet before throwing himself back onto the end of the couch.

Finally, Mom spoke. "We have some news to share with you, Khalil," she began. She rose from her seat and slowly approached me, taking my hands as she drew near. "For the past three years, you have been in trouble all the time. You have become a problem for this family, and we are afraid you are going to hurt someone really badly one day."

I dropped her hands and took a step back. "What are you talking about?" I asked. "I don't understand."

I heard a metallic clink nearby and looked over to see

the police officer unhooking the handcuffs from his belt.

"Am I being arrested?"

"We think it's best that you get help, son." The tears were running freely down Mom's face now.

"We?" I threw back at her angrily, searching her face for answers. When she didn't respond, I looked at the others. But no one would meet my eyes. Was my whole family feeding me to the wolves?

*This isn't really happening,* I told myself. Any moment now, someone would start laughing, or I'd wake up from this weird, disturbing nightmare.

"Just tell him the truth, Mom," Damien finally blurted impatiently from the side of the room. "Just tell him he is no longer wanted here."

"Shut your damn mouth, boy!" Mom shot back. "He will always be a part of this family, even if he doesn't live with us anymore."

I couldn't believe what was going down. They were actually sending me away.

At Mom's comment, Damien's anger erupted. "Enough with the lies!" he spat. Turning to me, he added,

"I can't believe you didn't see it. You are not really a part of this family. You're not one of us. You don't even look like us." His stare was fierce. As soon as he finished, an oddly satisfied look swept over his face, as if he were enjoying himself. But his comments only confused me.

"What?" I stared at him. "What's that supposed to mean? What do you mean I am not 'one of you?'" But he remained silent, still sporting a smug grin.

"We are going to miss you, Khalil," Mom stepped closer to me again, this time grasping my upper arm and giving me a gentle squeeze. A few of my siblings nodded in agreement with Mom's comment, but no one said anything. One by one, they stood up and filed out of the living room. Mom was the last to go, squeezing my shoulder again as she headed for the kitchen. I found myself alone in the living room with the police officer and a woman I had never met. Before I could ask another question, I was handcuffed and escorted out of the apartment.

"What did I do?" I pleaded with the police officer as we walked the short distance down the sidewalk to his cruiser.

Just then, the front door squeaked open loudly behind us. I looked over my shoulder to see Dakota running up to us. "Take this," she commanded, shoving her fist towards me. Inside was a thin silver necklace with a pendant in the shape of a half heart. She reached around and placed it in my cuffed hands. As she looked back up at me, I saw the tears in her eyes.

"Dakota, please, just tell me what I did," I begged. "I don't understand." I stared at her, searching her face for an answer. Before she could speak, though, Damien appeared in the doorway.

"Do you really want to know the truth?" he shouted, striding up to us. "I'll say what no one else will," he sneered. "*You were adopted, Khalil.* There it is. You are not and will never be a part of this family!" Giving me one final, contemptuous look, he grabbed Dakota by the wrist and pulled her back inside the apartment. Helplessly, she glanced briefly over her shoulder at me before he pulled her inside and slammed the door.

"Adopted? I'm adopted?!" I said aloud, my mind reeling. I stared back up at the house and saw Mom standing in front of her bedroom window, looking down at me. Or was she my mom? I wasn't sure anymore. Apparently, the only family I'd ever known wasn't even my own.

I knew I'd been acting out and behaving badly, but this was too much. I'd never imagined they'd send me away. And how was I supposed to handle discovering I wasn't even who I thought I was? I stood there, unmoving and dumbfounded, until the police officer tucked me into the back seat of his cruiser. Closing the door behind me, he joined the white woman up front and started the engine.

I looked out the window as we slowly pulled away from the place I'd always called home. I was shaken to the core. Everything I'd believed to be true - all the things I had accepted and never questioned about myself and my life - had all turned out to be lies. I didn't even know who I was.

"I'm sorry, kid," the officer said, looking back at me through the rearview mirror.

I stared back, my face blank, unable to process it all.

"In six short months, and with good behavior, there is a good chance that you can return home to your family."

The social worker shot me a half smile. "I believe in you."

*What family?* The thought came unbidden, and I pushed it away. I was angry, confused, and so very alone. I didn't even feel like I had myself to rely on anymore. Was anything about me true? Was Khalil even my real name? Was tomorrow actually my birthday? Or were even those things part of the lie?

Closing my eyes, I laid my head back against the seat and tried to shut it all out. By the time we reached our destination, I'd mostly succeeded. I felt numb, but I'd pulled myself together. As the police officer parked the cruiser, I looked out the window. The name emblazoned on the building in front of us read, "House of Hope."

# CHAPTER 7

**It was Tuesday morning** on one of the last days of summer, and the sun was just peeking over the horizon, staining the pale morning sky with orange streaks. I'd barely opened my eyes and was staring blearily out the window at the painted sky when Sanchez Howard stormed into my bedroom.

"Get up, and get dressed!" he shouted, grabbing my shoulders, and shaking me hard. "Those punks that challenged us the other day are out back."

I pushed him away. "How long have they been

waiting?" I asked as I swung my legs over the side of the bed and sat up.

"I don't know," he paced the small room. "Just get dressed."

"Give me ten minutes," I said.

"Ten minutes?" he grunted, obviously annoyed. "Who takes that long to clean their ass?"

"Just meet me in the lounge in ten minutes."

Rolling his eyes, he sauntered back across the small room. Pausing at the door, he looked over his shoulder and grinned back at me. "And don't play with yourself while you're in there, either. Gotta preserve that energy, KG."

Since my recent arrival at the House of Hope group home, I'd kept mainly to myself. I was a long way from the place I'd called home, but I'd learned enough before my "family" kicked me out to know it was better to play your cards close to your chest. We were in inner city Boston, and that meant most guys were either dealers or thugs involved in criminal activity.

Only Sanchez, one of the older kids who'd been at the home for a while, had tried to foster a relationship with me. I proceeded cautiously, ensuring anything I shared with him was insignificant. I knew better than to trust. It had gotten me in trouble before. Trusting made you vulnerable.

A few minutes later, we were headed out the door and towards the blacktop out back. I heard our challengers, Leon Pollack and Bryce Taylor, before I saw them, flinging insults and bragging about how they were going to destroy us.

Leon was tall, burly, and always smelled like expired lunch meat. He constantly walked around the group home as if he owned it. His counterpart, Bryce, was short, stocky and much lighter-skinned than Leon, with dirty dreadlocks that looked like they hadn't been washed in years. Rumor had it he was the best baller in the group home. But he'd never gone up against me before.

In fact, before today, no one at the group home had ever seen me ball, except Sanchez. I'd hit the court regularly in my old life, but I wasn't sharing anything with anyone here. I steered clear of the court, keeping my skills to myself. But I missed handling the ball, the sound of the game, and the confidence I felt on the court. So, I snuck outdoors one evening while everyone was watching TV in the lounge to work out the kinks and practice my skills. I was really in the groove, sinking three-point shots from all over the court, when Sanchez appeared out of nowhere. Impressed, he made me an offer I couldn't refuse - a pair of his Air Jordans if I teamed up with him to beat Leon and Bryce. I'd always wanted a pair, and he had about five, so I agreed. There was only one condition: I would only get the Jordans if we won.

I was going to make sure we won.

"Are you ready to take these clowns out?" Sanchez tossed out as he twirled the basketball on the tip of his right index finger.

*More than ready,* I thought, nodding in response as I bent to tighten the laces on my sneakers. They had definitely seen better days. Those new shoes are as good as mine.

"Give us a few minutes to warm up," Sanchez said, slamming the ball at Leon before kneeling to adjust the laces on the pair he'd chosen for today: his best black and white Air Jordans.

"We don't need to warm up," I told Sanchez loudly, watching the edges of the court fill up with more kids from the home. We were going to have plenty of spectators. Most of them cheered loudly for Leon and Bryce; Sanchez and I were the clear underdogs.

"Yeah, let's get this game started," Bryce shouted, chest-bumping Leon. "Chalk up another victory for the House of Hope's *only* undefeated team."

"Let's shoot for it," Leon suggested, passing to Sanchez.

"Nah," Sanchez tossed the ball to Bryce. "Your ball first."

"We don't need any charity," Bryce sneered, throwing the ball back to Sanchez.

"Okay," Sanchez shrugged and stepped behind the free throw line. "I tried to warn you." He dribbled, took his shot, and missed by a mile. He winked at me as the crowd jeered, booing loudly.

Bryce wistfully stepped up to the line and easily shot the ball straight into the net. "Our ball first, suckers!"

With the ball in play, the game began to roll fast. Leon and Bryce scored first.

"Good shot, Bryce," shouted Leon. I evened the score moments later. For the next twelve points, the game went back and forth, tying us up once more when I once again stole the ball from Leon and made a layup.

"Let's stop joking around and finish them off," I breathed to Sanchez as we jogged down the court. "And when we win, I want the Retro Jordans."

He grinned and nodded.

With new focus, we took our game up a notch. Even though it was our first time on the court together, it was as if Sanchez and I had teamed up countless times before. Every pass was perfect, and we sank every shot. In no time, we were winning twenty to twelve.

Sensing imminent defeat, Leon began to take the dirty route. As I dribbled past him, he swung his elbow at my face. I stepped back, narrowly missing the assault, and shot him a menacing look. "Watch your elbow."

"Whatever!" he shouted.

"Throw another elbow and see what happens," I threatened.

Despite being caught up in the moment, I should have known better than to threaten him. I hadn't been at the group home very long, but I'd heard about Leon's insanely short temper on my first day. As soon as the words were out of my mouth, Leon dropped the ball and charged me.

He'd been in plenty of fights before and knew where he was aiming. But it wasn't my first fight, either. At the last second, I stepped aside and took him in with a heavy right hook. He hit the ground like a jackhammer.

I hoped he'd have the good sense to stay down. But he immediately popped back up into a fighting stance. Without waiting, he charged me again. In a moment, we were surrounded, the crowd cheering as I sidestepped him again and again, delivering heavy blows every time. Focused as I was, I only vaguely noticed when the circle of onlookers parted to let a short, fat kid with large, protruding eyes stride towards us.

"Get off of him before I kill you!" he shouted, grabbing the back of my shirt, and flinging me across the court. The fat kid was far stronger than he looked. My body did a double barrel roll before I got my feet back under me and turned to face my new attacker. *How dare he!*

Incensed, I tightened my fists and charged at him, connecting an uppercut to his flabby chin. Unprepared for my intense assault, he dropped to his knees, curling into a fetal position with his arms over his face. But I wasn't done yet. I let loose blow after blow, pummeling every unprotected part of him. The watching crowd of kids screamed and punched the air, urging me on. There was so much adrenaline coursing through me, I never saw the staff members rushing forward to break up the fight.

Before I knew it, strong hands pinned my arms behind me, and I was roughly guided away from the blacktop.

It looked like I wasn't getting those Air Jordans after all.

Two hours later, I was sitting on a hard, armless chair outside the office of Mr. Tannerhill, the director of the group home. I didn't have to be a long-time resident to know it was not good to be called into the director's office.

Suddenly, Sanchez stuck his head around the corner. "What's going on?" he whispered with concern. "Everyone is talking about what happened on the basketball court today."

"Yeah, I know," I whispered back.

"Some people are saying you could've killed that little butterball."

"Yeah, well, whoever said that better watch out. They'll be next." I wasn't sure why his comment irked me, especially since I knew he was right. I'd pretty much lost it out there.

Just then, Mr. Tannerhill stepped out into the hallway, the heavy office door falling shut behind him. His face was grim. "We're ready for you, Khalil."

Sanchez shot me an encouraging look before turning away, but I could feel my heart slamming against my ribcage. The look on Mr. Tannerhill's face told me I was in a lot of trouble. However, before we stepped into his office, he turned and gave me an unexpected fatherly hug.

"Everything is going to be fine," he offered. But his reassurance felt uncertain. Looking down at me, he took a deep breath and opened the office door, ushering me in.

Seated at the small table in the corner was an attractive, well-dressed, white woman with long, curly, red hair that gently framed her face. She smiled kindly at me as I entered the office. A tall, stern man was standing next to her, dressed in black cargo pants and a short-sleeved gray polo shirt. For some reason, the two of them reminded me of David and Goliath.

Mr. Tannerhill positioned himself behind his desk as the red-haired woman greeted me. "Hi, Khalil. My name is

Susan Yearly, and I'm the social worker who has been assigned to your case."

"Case?" I blurted in bewilderment. A social worker was the last thing I'd expected. "What case?"

Before she could say another word, Goliath spoke, pulling a set of shiny, silver handcuffs from behind his back. "My name is Officer Terry, and you're under arrest for assaulting Leon Pollack and Blake Harden."

"Blake Harden?" I asked. "Who the hell is Blake Harden?" *Was that the butterball kid? He attacked me first!* I looked around the room, but no one answered me. Instead, the officer pulled my hands behind my back and snapped on handcuffs. As he silently walked me down the hallway and out the front door of House of Hope, I felt my anger rise again. Whoever Blake Harden was, I was going to make sure he paid for this.

# CHAPTER 8

**We arrived at the** police station, and by 4 p.m. I'd been booked and charged with assault and battery as Class A felonies. Then they took me to a tiny room and questioned me about the incident. I wanted to tell my side of the story to clear my name, but I knew all I had was my word against theirs. Saying something would likely just get me into more trouble, so I kept my mouth shut.

When they realized I wasn't talking, I was placed in a holding cell. The smell was horrid, more than I could bear. Feces covered the urinal and sidewalls. I tried to pick a spot on the dirt-laden mattress adjacent to the wall, but it also had spots of dried feces and urine on it. The only clean items inside the cell were a neatly folded blanket wrapped in clear plastic and a roll of toilet paper. I carefully wrapped my hands with some toilet paper, pulled the soiled mattress from the bed, and laid my blanket on top of the frame. Unsure what was coming next, I tried to get comfortable enough to rest, but one of the detainees in the cell across from me was screaming bloody murder, and the hours dragged on slowly. As night finally fell, his screeching ceased. But my thoughts kept swirling, leaving me awake long into the night.

The next morning, I was awoken by a uniformed security guard yanking open my cell door. Grabbing me roughly by the shoulder, he snapped on handcuffs before leading me down the hallway. With every step, I felt more like a criminal, but I put on a show of detachment, pretending to not be bothered.

He loaded me into the back of a police cruiser, and soon we pulled up in front of a large institutional building. The sign over the doors told me we were at the Juvenile and Domestic Relations District Court. As we walked in, my heart sped up, pounding frantically. A police officer pulled open a courtroom door as we approached. I spotted Mr. Tannerhill and Ms. Yearly already seated near the front of the room, awaiting my arrival. I hoped they would persuade the judge to send me back to the group home. I didn't want to end up in a youth detention center. Surviving there would be worse than surviving on the inner city streets. Besides, I still had a score to settle at House of Hope.

As we walked up to the front of the room, and Mr. Tannerhill's and Ms. Yearly's faces came into view, my gut twisted. Their expressions were pained, and even though I was sure they had heard us coming down the aisle, neither one of them would meet my eye.

I was unceremoniously pushed down into a seat in the front row next to a short, dark-skinned woman with curly, shoulder-length hair.

"Hi," she said, looking me over. There was little warmth in her eyes. "My name is Jasmine Dupree, and I am the attorney that will represent you today. I read your case file and believe I can convince the judge to give you only a five-year sentence in the Juvenile Corrections Reform Center."

My jaw dropped. "A five-year sentence?" I repeated, aghast. She'd said "only," as if five years were short, as if it could be much longer. *Was it really that bad? So what if I'd beat up a few guys. That happened all the time. Didn't it?*

Glancing over my shoulder, I quickly scanned the courtroom. Almost every seat was now full. I spotted Leon and a few other kids from House of Hope in a row near the back. *Are they here to testify against me?* Catching my eye, Leon threw me the middle finger. The others sniggered silently. I glared back.

Jasmine's low voice pulled me back around. "You can plead guilty and take this sentence," she stated calmly, "or you can be tried as an adult. So, what will it be?"

"Tried as an adult?" I repeated. "But I'm only thirteen!"

She looked me over once more and gave me a depreciating smile. "Five years will be a breeze for someone like you."

"What do you mean by *someone like me*?" I asked with a frown. Just then, I heard Mr. Tannerhill, seated behind me, praying aloud. He had his hands clasped and his head bowed.

"... Please watch over him, and please protect him while he is in jail," he whispered. "Protect your child from the murderers and rapists he will encounter while he's in there. In Jesus' name, I pray. Amen."

*What the hell?* Why wasn't he praying for some sort of leniency for me? How about, "Give him a second chance," or even, "Let my people go?" Anything would be better than that pathetic prayer.

"So, what's it going to be?" demanded my attorney, nudging my shoulder. "I have to tell the judge something."

"Listen," I sighed. It seemed like it was time for someone to hear my truth. The only truth, as far as I knew. "When I was led through the doors of the court this morning, I knew the deck was stacked against me. I'm a thirteen-year-old black male from the gutter who happens to be a part of a foster care system that doesn't give a damn about me. Please," I reached for her hand. Surprise flitted across her face. "I'm asking you to fight for me. You are all I have left." I searched her eyes, begging her to understand.

Before she could respond, the bailiff's voice rang across the courtroom. "All rise! The Honorable Judge Clarence D. O'Bryan is now presiding."

The judge surveyed the courtroom sternly before lowering himself behind the bench. "This court is now in session. Please be seated."

"This morning we are here for the case of Gilliam versus the Commonwealth of Massachusetts." Judge O'Bryan flipped through the docket, reviewing the contents. Glancing towards the front row, his blue eyes shot me a piercing look before shifting his gaze to my left.

"Attorney Dupree," he growled with a nod in her direction.

"Good morning, Your Honor. Permission to approach the bench?" He nodded, and she stepped quickly forward. She spoke in hushed tones, too quiet for me to hear. I waited nervously, bouncing my knee.

Turning back towards me, she met my eyes and winked, adding a tiny thumbs up even though her hands remained close to her sides. I felt a glimmer of hope. Maybe she was one of the good ones. Maybe I still had a chance of going back to the group home.

"So, what happened?" I whispered excitedly.

"I tried." She shrugged and slipped my case file back into her briefcase.

"What? What do you mean you tried?" I asked, agitated. "What did the judge say? What did you say?"

"Stand up," she said simply, ignoring my questions. "Judge O'Bryan is about to address the court."

Judge O'Bryan's deep voice interrupted our exchange, pinning me again with his sharp gaze. "Khalil Gilliam, you have been charged with two cases of assault and battery against minors."

From the back of the courtroom, I swore I could hear Leon and the others still sniggering at my expense.

"Your attorney tells me that you are pleading to lesser charges. Is that right?"

Attorney Dupree nudged me. "Say yes."

"Yes, Your Honor." But what was I agreeing to?

"Son, do you realize you could have killed these two young men? The only reason you are not being tried as an adult and spending the next twenty years of your life in a federal prison is because I believe there's still a chance you can turn your life around.

"But crimes of this severity cannot go unpunished. For your misdeeds, you will spend the next five years, or until your eighteenth birthday, inside the Massachusetts Juvenile Corrections Reform Center for Boys."

Still staring at me, he paused with his gavel suspended in midair. "Before we finish, the two young men that you assaulted are here today. Do you have anything to say to them?"

I turned and looked over my shoulder at the group of kids in the back row, all from House of Hope. Most of them wouldn't meet my eyes, other than Leon, who gave me a defiant grin. *That little punk,* I thought, clenching my hands into fists at my sides. There was no way I was apologizing to any of them. I wasn't sorry; they got exactly what they deserved. I turned back to Judge O'Bryan resolutely, keeping my mouth shut.

He dropped his gavel heavily, and the sound echoed ominously. I couldn't help but think it sounded a hell of a lot like a heavy, steel door closing on the rest of my life. Numbly, I sat there until a tall police officer with unbelievably huge arms pulled me up out of my seat and escorted me out of the courtroom, down the halls, out the front doors, and down the steps to his cruiser. In shock, I avoided making eye contact with anyone until I was seated in the back seat of the car and noticed the tall officer staring at me through the rearview mirror. As soon as he caught my eye, he spoke.

"You know the judge was trying to give you a way out, right?" he asked as he started the car. His voice was deep and surprisingly kind. "He probably would have lightened your sentence if you had apologized to those boys."

I wasn't sure where he was going with the father-figure angle. What business was it of his where I ended up? And what good did it do to tell me this now? I was already sentenced and being carted away. Remaining obstinately silent, I managed to avoid rolling my eyes. Instead, I broke away from his gaze and stared out the window. Shrugging, he pulled away from the curb and maneuvered the cruiser out into the street.

SECRETS BEGIN

As we drew closer to the Juvenile Corrections Reform Center, a sense of calm resignation slowly fell over me. Whatever was awaiting me at the Reform Center for the next five years, I would deal with it. I'd already been taunted, bullied, blamed, and abandoned. I'd survived it all and had come out stronger on the other side.

This time was no different.

# CHAPTER 9

**As much as I hated** to admit it, Attorney Dupree was right: My years spent at the juvenile detention center were a breeze. It turned out the show of bravado that originally earned me my reputation at school worked flawlessly on the kids at the Center, too. Minus a few initial scuffles with some of the wanna-be thugs, the other kids mostly just left me alone. It was actually a lot easier for me than living at home had been, dealing with bullying from both my brothers and my classmates.

As I settled into life at the Center, I found myself with

more time and energy on my hands than I'd ever had before. It turned out keeping up my tough-guy attitude around my family and at school had taken a lot of mental and emotional work to maintain. But with the kids at the Center already afraid of me, that facade had become largely unnecessary. I needed a distraction, something to occupy my time, or five years without a fight was going to be a real challenge.

Because of the severity of my crime, Judge O'Bryan assigned me to Mrs. Jacobsen, the center's psychologist, for daily counseling.

I'd always thought therapists were assigned to crazy people, but as the weeks flew by and the sessions continued, I realized I'd assumed wrong. I didn't think I was crazy, and Mrs. Jacobsen treated me like I was the brightest star in the sky.

"You have a bright future, Khalil," she told me one day from behind her desk. "Your past will not dictate your future. You will."

I couldn't help but doubt her. "Why do you care?" I finally asked with curiosity. "No one else does."

75

Her forehead creased, mirroring the pain on my own face. She rose from behind her desk and came to take the seat next to me. Looking into my eyes, she placed her hand on my shoulder. "Because you are worth it, Khalil. I believe in you."

Her words unlocked emotions I'd hidden so deeply I'd forgotten they were there. I wanted to trust her, badly. It just didn't seem safe. Small tears squeezed out of my eyes and fell in pairs down the sides of my face, and I looked away, trying to hide them.

"It's okay to cry," she rubbed my back in small circles, making the tears come faster. "It's safe here. Let it out, son."

So I did. I let it all come out. I cried and cried until I couldn't cry anymore. To my surprise, I felt a little better, lighter somehow.

That was the last day I cried in therapy. The next day, Mrs. Jacobsen decided to send me to the one place she knew I would never get in trouble, mostly because there were never any other kids there.

"You have a brilliant mind, Khalil." She handed me a

piece of paper. "I believe the library will be a good use of your time while here."

"What is this?" I looked down at the paper.

"Some very important books for you to read. Intellectually, I believe these books will take you to the next level."

The list was long, filled with names I didn't recognize and couldn't pronounce. "Who is Machiavelli? And Plato? What kind of name is Plato, anyway?"

She smiled. "They are the names of some of our world's greatest philosophers. Enjoy them. You will thank me later. Happy reading!"

Shrugging, I headed for the library, scanning the long list as I walked. Were there any authors on here I recognized? It wasn't until I reached the bottom that I found one: Ralph Ellison, the author of my favorite book, *The Invisible Man*. It was a story about a man who feels invisible thanks to the refusal of others to see him. Boy, could I relate! Maybe there were some other worthwhile books on this list, too.

I immersed myself in reading, absorbing every book I

could get my hands on. As I did, I quickly became the Center's greatest debater. No one, not even the staff, could match wits with me. I was discovering my mind was even more powerful than my fists.

Watching me tear through her list and then through the rest of the Center's small library, Mrs. Jacobsen told me she was petitioning the juvenile district court to grant me the opportunity to attend high school outside of the Center. A few days after sharing this news, she called me out of class.

I headed for her office, but before I could knock on the door, it flew open, revealing Judge O'Bryan. I hadn't seen him since the hearing that had landed me in the Center. I was immediately on edge.

"Good morning, Mr. Gilliam." He extended his right hand, and I cautiously shook it.

"Good morning, Your Honor."

"I have heard nothing but great things about you from Mrs. Jacobsen. I hear you are the captain of the Center's debate team, and one hell of a basketball player."

"Yes sir," I smiled widely. I was proud of both accomplishments.

He flipped open his portfolio and handed me an envelope. "Open it."

I hesitated for a moment before accepting it. Feeling all eyes on me, I slowly opened the envelope and read the contents, my eyes widening more with every line. "Thank you, sir!" I grinned at him and Mrs. Jacobsen. "I will not let either of you down."

"I knew there was something great in you," the judge said, shaking my hand one final time before exiting the office.

Clutching the letter that contained my future, I slowly made my way back to my room. Sitting on the bed, I reread the letter again, trying to absorb it fully. Judge O'Bryan had agreed to Mrs. Jacobsen's petition for me to attend high school outside of the Center, and I would be starting at Lakewood High School next week. All my hard work had paid off. I knew this was my chance at redemption, and I was going to take full advantage of the opportunity.

With my dedication to my studies, high school classes were a breeze. Though I was only sixteen, at Mrs.

Jacobsen's suggestion, I began reaching out to colleges and universities all over the country. The initial conversations were almost all positive; a few schools even verbally extended full academic scholarships. Riding high, I submitted application after application, excited about all the options I would have once I was accepted. I'd been cast away by my family like trash, but now I was wanted. It felt like a dream come true.

Once I submitted my applications, I resigned myself to waiting for the official responses. When the first one arrived, I tore it open instantly, my eyes scanning for confirmation of my acceptance. But... no. They were sorry, my criminal history precluded my admission.

*How could they, after all they promised me?* Angrily, I tore the letter into tiny pieces before tossing it in the trash.

The next day, the second letter arrived. *Surely this school will see reason.* But its contents were the same - they were "unable" to admit me because of my past. Crumpling the paper in my fist, I threw the tightly wadded ball across the room.

Within the span of a week, my dream devolved into a nightmare. It seemed no one could see past my past. One by one, the same colleges that had marveled about me rescinded their offers, leaving me, once again, abandoned.

The last letter arrived early in the day, while I was out behind the building shooting hoops, trying to blow off some steam. A few kids were hanging around nearby, but as usual, they were giving me a wide berth. Just then, Mrs. Jacobsen strode up to the side of the court and beckoned to me.

"What did he do this time?" a fat kid whispered loudly.

"I don't know, but it has to be bad if the blue-eyed witch has summoned him to her dungeon," another kid replied. Everyone laughed. "See you in hell, Khalil!" he called.

Rolling my eyes, I headed off the court, trailing behind Mrs. Jacobsen until we reached her office. She ushered me through the door.

"Have a seat," she instructed crisply, making her way behind the desk, and sitting down.

I sat, but I folded my arms across my chest, eying her warily.

"So, what's the plan?" she asked, staring at me.

"What do you mean, 'the plan?'"

"I mean, what's next for Khalil Gilliam?"

Was this some sort of trick question? She knew just as well as I did that I'd been rejected everywhere; I'd told her about each letter as it arrived. Now, with all my scholarship applications denied, I had no real next move.

"Maybe find a job," I tossed back.

"What about college?"

My eyes flashed. "You already know the answer to that. Just like always," I reminded her, "nobody wants me."

"Is that so?" She raised her eyebrows, then withdrew a manila envelope from a drawer. She tossed it on the top of the desk in front of me.

I slowly opened the envelope and removed the letter. It was from a small, four-year college in Manchester, New Hampshire. Not only had they accepted my application, but they were also offering me a full academic scholarship.

"Congratulations, Khalil," she smiled. "But that's not the only good news I have for you. The judge also signed this order releasing you from juvenile custody a year early. I'm so proud of you, Khalil. You made it. You are wanted."

# CHAPTER **10**

**On my seventeenth birthday,** I was released from the youth detention center. As a minor with nowhere to go until I started college, I reluctantly moved back into my old family home.

I was hardly the same person I'd been when I left, but that didn't stop the frustration I felt concerning my brothers. One moment they acted as if we were tight, and the next they were bringing down hell. The only thing that kept me from going insane was remembering I was leaving soon. College was less than a month away and there was no way I was going to jeopardize my freedom.

The morning my family was supposed to take me to school, my resolve was once again put to the test. Damien stormed into our bedroom before I was even awake. I'd spent all night tossing and turning in anticipation of leaving.

"Let's go, Black Boy!"

"I'll be right there," I mumbled from the bed. Staring up at the cracks in the ceiling, I took one last look at what I was about to leave behind, which wasn't much, especially considering my family.

"Hurry up, we don't have all day. We're waiting on you, so get your ass in gear."

My anger flared. My older brothers had bullied me all my life, but it was my last day with them, and I was not going to get punked today.

"I'll be ready when I'm ready," I retorted, my voice dripping with disrespect. But the resulting gleam in his eye told me I should have known better than to get smart with him even if it was my last day at home. With three long strides, he was next to my bed.

"What did you say, Black Boy?" He yanked me out of the bed and onto my feet, then immediately unloaded a punishing blow to my chest, sending me to the floor.

"Nothing," I replied, slowly getting up and dusting myself off. I could feel the bile rising in my throat, but I kept my cool. Punching him in the face was not worth going to prison.

"Thought so!" He strutted out of the room.

I turned to gather the handful of remaining things that weren't already packed, grabbing my backpack from the floor at the foot of my bed. As I turned back around, I noticed Damien still standing in the doorframe, eyeing me while cracking his knuckles.

"If you're not ready in ten seconds, Black Boy, I'm going to make you wish you were never born."

Refusing to engage, I turned my back on him and rolled my eyes. The way he threw around the term "Black Boy" had always irritated me, though it was usually reserved for days when Damien knew being an asshole would get me riled up. But I wasn't going to let it phase me today.

Grabbing the last items and zipping them in, I slung the backpack over my shoulder and headed for the door.

"You got issues, man. You got some serious issues," I told him as I brushed past him down the hall.

I'd overslept; it looked like everyone else was already in the car. The house was quiet as I made my way past the kitchen and through the living room. As I stepped out of the apartment, I paused just outside the door, feeling a sudden rush of trepidation surge through me. Was this really happening? Here I was, a seventeen-year-old black male from Roxbury, Massachusetts, on my way to college. Who would have ever guessed I would make it out of the hood? And like this?

I turned to look back one more time, but Damien was right behind me. He leaned over and playfully jabbed me in the arm, cracking a smile.

"I'm sorry for not visiting you." He stepped out and closed the door behind him, then turned and threw his arm around my neck. "And for all the times I bullied you, too. I know I haven't been the best brother considering everything you've gone through over the years. None of us has. Please forgive us. We're all sorry."

It was the first apology I had ever heard from any of them. I wanted to believe him, but there was no way it was sincere. If any of them had cared at all, they'd have shown up when it mattered. Had they? No. Not once.

*To hell with him and his apology.* I headed for the car. The more I thought about it, though, the angrier I got. How dare he try and apologize for everything he'd done - they'd *all* done - so casually, as if it had been nothing? I shoved my anger down, putting on my best poker face. But I could still feel the intensity boiling inside.

I couldn't recall being this worked up since the day I'd whipped Blake Harden back at the House of Hope. It was his fault I'd been sent to the Center in the first place. Recalling the incident fueled the fire inside me. That fat little punk had started something he hadn't been prepared to finish. I would make sure it was finished, though. Someday, somehow, Blake Harden would pay for what he'd done.

In the meantime, though, I had Damien and my family to deal with. I just needed to hold it together long enough to get to school. I knew I wanted more than what the streets could offer, and this scholarship was my ticket out. Besides, after everything I'd survived so far, college would surely be a cakewalk.

As we neared the car, Damien grabbed my arm, pulling us to a halt. I hitched my backpack higher on my shoulder, trying to get a better hold on everything I was carrying. He waited until I looked up at him.

"Look, are you really sure you're ready to take this giant leap of faith?" he asked skeptically.

I stared at him, incredulous. Was that really what he thought? Did he understand nothing?

"Faith?" My voice cracked, but I held back the tears. "You think I'm leaving because I'm taking a leap of faith? No. No way. Was it faith that led my birth parents to give me up for adoption? Faith that put me with a family that also gave me up? Faith that landed me in a youth detention center? No. I'm leaving because I don't have another choice, do I?" I was practically screaming now. My heart was racing, and I was breathing fast; I took a deep breath and let it out slowly.

"Are you kidding me, man?" Damien slapped me in the back of the neck. "You always have a choice, Black Boy." Oddly, his unexpected gesture and comment seemed to calm me somewhat.

I frowned and rubbed the back of my neck. "You play too much."

"Trust me, I will be the least of your problems, college boy."

"What is that supposed to mean?"

"In time, you'll see." He nudged me hard enough that I stumbled, which made him start laughing. If he kept this up, there was a real chance I'd lose it before we reached the school. Regaining my footing, I headed for the trunk of his car, glancing around to see if anyone I knew was watching. But there was no one around other than my impatient, mocking family. It looked as if my departure would go unnoticed. That was a relief. Slamming the trunk of Damien's rusted, powder blue Chevy Nova closed, I sighed. I was not looking forward to arriving on campus in this heap.

Damien thought his car was a lady magnet, and none of us in the family dared tell him differently. But there had been plenty of times when, cruising around the neighborhood, I intentionally leaned my seat far back enough to be out of sight. After all, in the "hood" you never knew when you might roll up on a pretty girl or someone from your crew. I did not want to be spotted in my brother's so-called pimpmobile.

In addition to being anything but a lady magnet, Damien's car was also unpredictable. We all sat and waited as he tried to get the car started, but the engine refused to turn over. Ten minutes later, after countless failed attempts, the engine wrestled its way to life, and we were finally on our way.

# CHAPTER 11

**As we proceeded** down Mount Pleasant Avenue, I took one last look out the window. Challenging as it had been at times, this neighborhood had been the only home I'd really known. But now, the basketball court where I'd spent countless hours would be dominated by another. Any closeness I'd shared with my family and friends would become part of my past, and I would be on my own.

I looked around the car, my family crammed inside. Mom sat up front between Damien and Stephon. I could see the joy fill her eyes every time she looked at each of us.

Michelle played patty cake with Dakota beside me in the back. Damien was fighting to roll down his window. And Stephon sat expressionless, as usual. Messed up as we were, we were a family.

Suddenly, the thought struck me: *How would I make it without them?* They were all I had. Sure, I'd spent my years at the Center away from them. And yes, I'd been adopted. But that didn't change the years we'd already shared. Now, without them and without the structure of life at the Center, what would happen?

It was a blisteringly hot day, and Damien's car did not have air conditioning. As the sun beat down and baked the car, beads of perspiration popped out on my forehead, quickly accumulating to run down my forehead and the sides of my face. My shirt was slowly becoming soaked. It didn't help that we were packed skin-to-skin in the car, and for some reason, the back windows were still up. With my thoughts churning and the temperature rising, I desperately needed some cool air, so I tried to roll down the window closest to me, pulling at the old-school winding crank. But it would not budge. Then I recalled that I had never actually seen the rear windows down. I gave up and returned to gazing at the traffic on the highway, sweat beads clinging to my forehead.

As we neared New Hampshire, though, I began to panic. What had I been thinking? There was no way I was ready to be on my own. I needed a way out. I ran my fingers through my afro repeatedly until Stephon turned and stared at me coldly. Dropping my hand, I stifled a hard shiver.

*He's jealous,* I told myself, turning to look out the window and trying to brush off his penetrating stare. I couldn't blame him for wanting to be in my spot. But it wasn't my fault he and Damien had both dropped out of school in the eleventh grade. At least at school I'd be away from Stephon. *Maybe attending college out-of-state was the right decision after all.* With this thought, I relaxed a little bit.

"Hey, Black Boy, we're in New Hampshire!" Damien blurted as we crossed the state line. He cranked the music up louder.

*Who was he calling Black Boy?* He wasn't too far

from blue himself. My anger, which had been simmering just below the surface, rose sharply.

"Ignorant mother..." I growled loudly, not caring who heard me. Everyone in the car began to laugh. The laughter was all the motivation Damien needed, and he continued clowning me, raucous laughter following every jibe.

Reminding myself to stay calm and ignore them, I looked out the window just in time to read a sign that said, "Welcome to New Hampshire - Live Free or Die."

*Live free or die?* I raised my eyebrows. Fat chance of that. As a young black man, I knew I could never be free in white America. Thinking about what "live free or die" really meant for my race and for me fueled my anger more. Who did they think they were, plastering up a sign like that?

Far as I could see, New Hampshire wasn't that different from Boston. White people had the best jobs, attended the best schools, and had the best education. Black people were just "niggers." The only time a white person had ever ventured into my neighborhood was during elections or to arrest someone, and the history books I studied in school taught more about slavery than equal rights. After four hundred years of slavery, could a black person ever really "live free" in white America?

"Khalil, are you scared?" Michelle's question brought me back to the present. It was the first thing she had said to me all morning. All eyes landed on me, and silence fell over the car. It seemed her question was one everyone wanted to know the answer to.

"Scared of what? I am not scared of anything!" Truth was, I was more than scared. I was terrified. I could feel my mask, the tough facade I'd cultivated for years, slipping out of place. I decided to take a page out of Stephon's book. Wiping all emotion from my face, I sat there, perfectly still, facing forward.

"Black Boy! We're here!" Damien yelled. I looked out the window once more, this time spotting a sign announcing Haysville College. Dragging the back of my hand across my forehead to wipe away the sweat, I hoped my family couldn't feel my fear.

Mom dug through her purse for the map the school

had mailed with my acceptance letter and began to direct Damien to Lowell Street. As we slowly cruised the campus streets, Damien, ever the ringleader, ripped into me once more.

"I don't know why you chose to go to this white school, Black Boy. You better keep one eye open when you sleep."

Did Damien know something about Haysville that I didn't? What did he mean I had better keep one eye open?

"We're here, Khalil." Michelle looked at me intently. "Are you sure you're not scared?"

I poked out my chest and squared my shoulders, trying to look courageous. "Scared of what? I already told you they better be scared of me."

"There it is! Lowell Street is right there!" Dakota yelled loudly enough for all of Manchester to hear. I sat upright, gripping the edge of the seat hard with both hands. As Damien searched for a space to park, I anxiously scanned the faces walking by the dormitory for another black face. *Not one.* It looked like I was all alone.

# CHAPTER 12

**Despite its fresh,** green beauty, Manchester was all white — pretty much the polar opposite of Roxbury. As I stared out the window, my mind was in overdrive. What was this place? What would happen to me here, one black face among a multitude of white ones? How would people look at me? What would I do if a white person called me nigger?

Damien parked the car, and my family piled out. There was no turning back. But now that I knew exactly how much of a minority I would be here, I was not looking forward to it.

"Hey, Black Boy," Damien snickered, "your friends, the KKK, are waiting for you."

My whole family exploded with laughter. Even Stephon had a rare grin on his face.

Noticing my frustration, Mom reached over and kissed me lightly on the cheek. Damien and my sisters continued to crack jokes about handing me over to the KKK.

"All right, Black Boy, let's get going!" Damien finally laughed. "Your Nazi friends are waiting for you."

I wasn't sure why Damien had suddenly decided he was a comedian; he'd never said a funny thing in his life. Now he thought he was Martin Lawrence. But he'd chosen the wrong time for it.

"You're not funny, Damien," I scowled.

"I'm not the one you need to get tough with, Black Boy. You better watch your back." As he popped the trunk and pulled out my luggage, I did a quick inspection of the nearby campus layout.

"What the hell have I gotten myself into?" I whispered under my breath.

As I grabbed my suitcases, I heard an unfamiliar male voice.

"Do you need any help?"

I turned, and to my surprise, I was met by another black face. The sight of him set me at ease so much that the fresh, New Hampshire air suddenly seemed even fresher and more invigorating. *Maybe there's hope after all.*

"What's up?" I said, extending my hand.

"What's up, man?" He shook my hand. "My name is Denzel."

"Good to meet you, Denzel. Khalil."

Denzel was a brown-skinned brother from Salem, Massachusetts. Built like a bodybuilder, Denzel seemed to have picked his clothes from the most recent style catalog. He looked like he had walked right out of a GQ magazine.

Before I could respond, I saw Stephon headed towards us, and for the first time all day, he spoke.

"Call me if any of these white boys try anything," he offered, then walked away, not waiting for a response.

I shrugged at Denzel. In response, he grabbed one of the suitcases, and we headed towards Lowell Hall with my family trailing behind us. Our conversation came easily. Before I knew it, he was bragging about how good an athlete he was.

"I played point guard on our state championship basketball team, and I was also the star running back on the football team," he finished.

"Is that right?" I said, impressed.

"What school did you go to?" he asked.

"Lakewood High, in Boston."

"Did you play any sports?"

"Yeah, I played basketball."

"Oh, yeah? How did your team do?"

"We did alright," I said. Our team had sucked, but I couldn't admit that. It sounded like Denzel had enjoyed an amazing high school experience, and there was no way I could match accolades with him. So, I did the next best thing and changed the subject.

A few moments later, we entered Lowell Hall, and a dark-haired, white boy with a lean frame approached us.

"Who's the white boy?" I asked, struggling to get a better hold on my suitcase.

"He's the resident director of Lowell Hall."

Dropping my suitcase, I walked up to him and took his extended hand in mine.

"Hello, my name is John Daniels," he said. "I'm the resident director here at Lowell Hall."

"It's nice to meet you, John. My name is Khalil Gilliam."

He opened a manila envelope and removed a sheet of paper with a long list of names on it. He searched the list and found my name at the very bottom of the page.

"You'll be staying in room number thirty-two, on the third floor." He handed me a set of keys. "Go through the door at the very top of the stairwell and take the first right. Welcome to Haysville."

"Thanks," I said, accepting the keys and looking towards the stairwell. Gathering up my bags again, my family and I headed off to find my room.

When we got to the top of the stairs, I noticed two white boys standing in the doorway of my room.

"What's up?" I gritted on the two of them as I headed in. Inside I found three beds, two of which were already made. I turned to the two white boys, "This is room thirty-two, right?"

"Yes. You must be Khalil," the taller one smiled.

"Yeah, that's right."

"We're your roommates," they said in unison.

"Wait - what?"

# CHAPTER 13

**Sharing a room with** Damien and Stephon had been bad enough. Now I had to share a room with two white boys — two white strangers. Reluctantly, I introduced myself.

"Nice to meet you. I'm Brian, and this is Paul."

Brian was six-foot-two and had dark, curly hair. His medium frame and muscular build suggested that he was an athlete of some kind. Paul was short and stocky and sported a buzz cut. He wore a pair of tight-fitting blue jeans and a white V-neck t-shirt that exposed the top part of his hairy chest.

"Do you need any help?" they asked, looking past me to where my family stood clustered in the hallway.

"Nah, I'm good." I walked past the two of them. From the doorway, Mom noticed my rudeness and gave me the evil eye, but I ignored her. The last thing I'd had in mind was sharing a room with two white boys.

As soon as I'd set my things down, Mom and my sisters swarmed in and began putting my belongings away.

"Hey, boy, make sure you wash your underwear. You know how you can get," Mom said loudly as she dangled my white briefs in the air. Dakota and Michelle couldn't bite back their laughter and giggled at her comment.

*Great,* I thought. Not even an hour on campus, and my family was already going to make me the school joke. I quickly grabbed my briefs and stuffed them into my pants pocket.

"Stop playing, Mom," I said sourly before walking out of the room, embarrassed.

I headed toward the stairs and heard Mom's voice ring across the hall as she called after me, "Boy, what's wrong with you?"

"Nothing is wrong!" I called back through gritted teeth.

Damien decided to add his two cents. "Mom, he's just mad because he's got to share a room with two white boys."

"Shut up, Damien, I'm not mad at nothing." I burned with embarrassment. Just then, my two sisters came out into the hallway, too, laughing uncontrollably. Apparently, Stephon had come into the room and threatened Brian and Paul.

Ignoring them, I refocused my attention on Mom. She seemed happy, and I knew I had to ride this one out even if it meant swallowing my pride.

I grabbed her hand and reassured her, "I won't let you down, Mom." She smiled back with tears in her eyes.

I headed back into the room to unpack the rest of my things. As I put the last of my stuff away, I overheard Mom behind me, talking to Brian and Paul. As if things were not bad enough already, Mom proceeded to open a Tupperware bowl full of fried chicken and offer them some. I looked at my mother as if she had lost her mind.

To my dismay, they both accepted. Paul sank his teeth into the chicken and smiled.

"I love me some fried chicken," he announced.

"Well, there is plenty more where that came from," Mom replied, removing a zip lock bag from her purse and slipping a few pieces inside. "I'll leave these for later."

Unable to watch the scene unfold any longer, I dropped what I was doing and walked out of the room for a second time.

Minutes later, Brian and Paul walked past me as I was sitting in the hallway, sulking.

"We're going dorm hopping. See you when we get back," Paul said. I got up and headed back into the room, disgusted by my family's behavior.

"All of your things are neatly put away," Mom said. Then, she grabbed my hand and looked me in the eyes.

"Baby," she wrapped her arms around me, "I know I haven't been the best mother to you. I hope you can forgive me. Everything you have endured in your young life has brought you to this moment, and I'm so proud of you. You are a wonderful son. One day, God is going to use you to help so many people. I love you so much, baby."

The sincerity of her words crept through my defenses,

reaching my heart. I felt the anger and resentment I'd harbored for so many years melt just a little.

Barely keeping my emotions in check, I smiled at her. "I love you too, Mom."

Quietly slipping me a fifty-dollar bill, she grasped my hand hard, then rallied the others to leave.

"Well, baby, we're going to get out of here now. Call us if you need anything." There were tears in her eyes.

"Don't worry, Mom, I'll be alright. I'll make sure I call you every day."

"You don't have to call every day, Black Boy. Give us some time to miss you," Damien joked. This time I laughed it off, following them down the hall to the exit.

As we approached the car, I hugged everyone except Stephon. I didn't want him getting nostalgic and trying to squeeze in a last-minute punch to the head for old times' sake.

Instead, I stood a distance away from him and said, "I'm going to miss you, Stephon."

He gave me a stoic look and nodded in return.

"Be strong, man, and don't let these white boys try to

punk you." He turned and walked towards the car without another look back.

"I won't."

It was tough watching my family get back into the car, knowing they were leaving me. But I also knew the longer they stayed, the harder it would be for me to say goodbye.

"I'll give you a call tonight," I promised.

"Okay, baby, we love you," Mom said, blowing me a kiss as Damien started the car.

Rolling down his window, Damien called out one final time. "Hey, Black Boy, remember what I told you - stay out of trouble, and don't be messing around with those white girls!"

I stood there listening to their laughter until I could no longer hear it. Then I kept watching until they turned the corner. Once I could no longer see them, I headed back inside Lowell Hall, wondering what my next move would be.

# CHAPTER 14

**School registration was** a couple days away, and since I didn't exactly have a plan to do anything, I decided to see what Manchester had to offer a young brother from the hood.

As I made my way down to the second floor, I heard someone singing. Following the noise, I reached the doorway of Denzel's room. In addition to singing loudly, he was dancing around and cleaning. But what really grabbed my attention was the one, lone bed in the room. Where were his roommates?

"What's up, Denzel? Where are your roommates?"

He continued to dance around the room, sporting a silly grin. "I don't have a roommate. This is my room," he said.

What did he mean by his room? How was that possible?

"How did you manage to avoid getting a roommate?"

He continued dancing. "I just asked for it when I arrived. There's another one on your floor, right across from your room."

"What? There is?" I could barely contain the excitement in my voice.

"Yeah, the guy who was going to move in decided to take a room downstairs with his high school buddy. Why don't you ask if you could get it?"

"Who should I ask?"

"Ask the Dean of Student Affairs. I met her earlier today. She's very cool, and I heard she likes brothers, too. And you know what they say about white girls. 'Once you go black, you never go back,' right?"

"Is that what they say?" I chuckled.

"That's what they say. The Dean is in the building

across the street on the eighth floor."

That was all I needed to hear. "Thanks, I'll fill you in later."

When I arrived at the Dean's office, there were a number of other students there. Could they all be here for the same reason as I was? Reluctantly, I sat down to wait next to a tall, slender, white boy.

"Hey, dude." He flashed a smile. Not in the mood for small talk, I ignored him. There were more pressing matters on my mind.

After an agonizingly long wait, a petite, white woman with short, brown hair finally approached me.

"Hi, I'm Dean Anthony. What can I do for you?"

I jumped to my feet. "I'm Khalil Gilliam, a freshman. I just arrived today." I was nervous, twirling my thumbs frantically. "There's a single room in Lowell Hall on the third floor, and it's vacant. Is there any chance I could get it?"

She rubbed the bottom of her chin with her hand. "Well Mr. Gilliam, if no one is listed as having the room by noon today, then I don't see why you couldn't have it."

I looked at the clock on the wall. It was five minutes before noon. Could my anxiety get any worse? *Why can't she just say yes?* But what was five minutes? I decided to assume it was a done deal.

"Great!" I exclaimed, already preparing my farewell speech for Brian and Paul.

"Wait just a minute, Mr. Gilliam. Weren't you assigned a room upon arrival? What's wrong with that one?"

I decided my best bet was to lay it on thick. "Listen, Dean Anthony, all of my life, I've had to share a room with my two older brothers. I just want something that I can call my own. I hope you understand."

"Completely. If it's okay with your resident director, it's okay with me." She extended her hand.

"Thank you," I smiled. Before she could change her mind, I scurried back to Lowell Hall. John was in the entryway chatting with Denzel when I arrived.

"Dean Anthony said if the vacant room on the third floor is still empty by noon today, then it's mine," I blurted.

"The room is still empty. You can move in right away," confirmed John.

After grabbing my new keys from him, I ran upstairs. Speeding into my old room, I interrupted Brian and Paul chatting. I could hardly wait to share my good news.

"I hate to be the bearer of bad news," I started.

"What happened?" Paul interrupted, concerned.

"The bad news is I will no longer be your roommate."

"Why?" they asked in unison.

"I have my own room now. It's right across the hall."

"That's totally rad, dude." Paul proclaimed. He smiled at Brian. "Do you need any help moving your stuff?"

"Nah, I can handle it," I said. It took several trips, but as I lugged my stuff across the hall, the grin never left my face. Now that I had some space to myself, this college thing was going to be alright.

# CHAPTER 15

**It took a week** for me to really settle in and start feeling like Haysville was no longer foreign territory. The girls on campus took an instant liking to my baby face and no-nonsense Boston swag. I was a hit, and I quickly embraced my newfound popularity.

One evening, I was watching the Boston Celtics game in the student lounge of Lowell Hall when Denzel, Kadeem Wilson, and James Childs stormed in from dorm hopping. Haysville had recruited the three of them to play basketball, and they were pretty good. Of course, I had the skills to beat them all and had been destroying them on the blacktop since we'd arrived on campus. But there had been no college recruiters at the detention center. Besides, my violent past precluded me from participating in team sports while I was locked up. Grateful as I was for the academic scholarship that had been my ticket out, it meant I'd have to prove myself to earn one of the prized walk-on spots on Hayville's basketball team.

"Man, you should have been there," Kadeem plopped down in a chair in the corner of the lounge and cracked open a Budweiser.

"How did you get beer?" I asked.

He fished something out of his pants pocket and held it up with a grin. "This fake ID, kid."

As the three of them discussed their dorm-hopping conquests and bragged about which of the girls they'd met, my almost-roommate Brian poked his head into the student lounge.

"Hey, guys. There's a keg party upstairs. Come on, free beer."

"Let's go crash the party!" Kadeem stood.

"Hell yeah!" Denzel and James rang in unison.

I grabbed my keys from the table in front of me and followed the guys towards the exit. Before we reached the door, though, a beautiful young woman strolled in.

"Hey, Denzel." She greeted him with a perfect smile. "Are you guys leaving?"

Suddenly, crashing the party was no longer important.

"How do you know Denzel?" Kadeem inquired.

"Our high school football teams are rivals. I've known Denzel for years. My name is Katrina." She extended her hand.

"It's nice to meet you, Katrina. My name is Kadeem, and I'm from Staten Island. Haysville offered me a full scholarship to play basketball. I'll probably start at small forward or shooting guard," he bragged.

"I'm James, and I was also recruited to play ball."

"You already know me," Denzel said.

"And who are you?" she smiled. "Another one of Haysville's recruits?"

"Nah, but I plan to try out for the team. I'm Khalil, but my friends call me KG."

For the next hour or so, Katrina, Denzel, Kadeem, and James drank beer Kadeem had brought and chatted about the upcoming school year.

"Denzel, wake me up when the Celtics game is over." I was feeling relaxed as I propped my feet up on the coffee table in front of me and flung my arms behind my head, ready for a catnap. Just then, Katrina came over.

"Mind if I sit here?"

"It's a free country." I said, to sound tough. "Sit anywhere you want."

"Thanks, KG." She plopped down on the couch, closed her eyes and laid her head on my shoulder.

*Damn, she is fine,* I thought, taking in the fragrance of her.

"Denzel?" I called out a second time.

"What's up?" He was now laying in the middle of the floor with his eyes closed.

"Did I ever tell you I'm a boxer?"

"I know how to box, too," Katrina chimed in, tilting her head on my shoulder to look up at me. "I can take you," she added confidently.

117

"You can take me?" I laughed. "I don't fight girls."

"What? Are you afraid this little girl will kick your ass in front of all your boys?" she sneered.

Hearing this, James, Kadeem, and Denzel whistled and began to cheer her on. I rolled my eyes, but the louder they cheered, the more smug she became. Without warning, she unleashed a left hook towards my jaw, barely missing.

"Are you crazy?" I demanded, shocked at the unexpected assault. "Your drunk ass almost hit me." She didn't respond, so I grabbed my keys from the table and stood, heading for the exit. Before I could reach the door, she caught up with me and took another swing at my jaw, again only missing by inches.

"Chill out, girl." I grabbed her by the wrists. "I don't have time for your games." She tussled violently to free herself, so I let her go. I'd no more than released her hands when she hurled yet another combination at me. By this point, Kadeem, James, and Denzel were all on the floor, laughing hysterically.

Though I managed to avoid every assault, her drunken

tirade was starting to piss me off. I wanted to knock this lunatic the hell out, but my mother had raised me not to hit girls, so I kept evading. Finally, I'd had enough, so I put her in a headlock. Unfortunately, it seemed it wasn't her first time in the position because I'd no more than gotten my arm around her neck when she reached back, grabbed my balls, and squeezed.

Ignoring Denzel and Kadeem, who both had tears in their eyes from laughing so hard, I decided it was time to stop playing fair. Leveraging my height and size, I grabbed her around the waist and lightly slammed her down on the sofa, somehow managing to free myself along the way.

But before I could stand back up, Katrina wrapped her arms around my neck, looped her leg around mine, and pulled me forcibly towards her until my hips rested firmly against hers. As soon as our bodies touched, time seemed to slow down. We lay there gazing into each other's eyes, our lips inches apart until I suddenly became aware of the others in the room. Letting her go, I got up, still holding her gaze. She rose too, and, despite our audience, moved in closer to trace the side of my face gently. Before I could register what was happening, she closed the gap between us and kissed me. It was the first time I had ever kissed a woman.

The laughing stopped, and no one in the room uttered a single word. A few moments later, she pulled away, staring at me.

James was the first to speak. "Are you okay, KG?"

"Yeah, I'm good." I broke away from her and headed for the door to the student lounge.

"Where are you going?" she asked, following me closely.

"Outside. To get some fresh air. Why, you want to roll?" Behind her, Kadeem and James watched in silence.

"Yeah, I'll go with you."

I looked back at Kadeem, James and Denzel, smiling to myself at the sight of their jaws hanging open. Then Katrina and I swept out of the student lounge.

# CHAPTER 16

**The day had finally arrived.** It was time to distinguish the professionals from the amateurs. Basketball tryouts were happening, and I was ready.

I was stretching at the other end of the court when Denzel, James, and Kadeem strolled into the gym. As school recruits, they would be supporting the tryout process for walk-ons. There were only a few walk-on spots available, but I wasn't worried.

"You ready?" James acknowledged me with a fist bump. I nodded. I had my eyes on last year's starting point guard, Carson Maine, the so-called best point guard Haysville had ever recruited. It was time to show him there was a new sheriff in town.

Just then, the gym's double doors flew open, and in walked Coach Gray, wearing a crisp, black suit.

"Everyone on the line," he shouted, pulling Carson forward from the group. "For those of you who are new to Haysville, this is Carson Maine, captain and leader of this team. He was last year's leading scorer. And, as I didn't recruit a lot of talented point guards this year, he will lead this year's team in scoring."

"Ha. He'll be eating those words in no time," I said under my breath. James, who happened to be standing next to me, raised his eyebrows in response.

"There are only twelve opening spots on this year's team, and ten of those are already taken." Coach Gray scanned the crowded gym. "That means at least sixty of you will not make it. So, give me everything you've got. Let's get things going."

At his direction, we formed ten lines and started running drills. By the time Coach Gray blew his whistle an hour later, we were all sucking wind.

"Everybody on the end line!" he shouted a second time. "You guys are in horrible shape. Horrible, horrible, horrible shape. We've got a lot of work to do, but first, we'll take a quick break."

He was right about people being out of shape. As soon as he released the room, several people dropped to the floor, holding their sides and grimacing at the cramping pain. Others dry heaved, trying to stay on their feet. The remainder of the group raced for the water fountain, seeking quick relief.

"This fat bastard is trying to kill us." I was winded, too, though not as badly as most of the guys in the gym. Hearing my comment, Denzel grinned over at me.

"What are you smiling for?" He was the only one in the room who looked like he wasn't close to death.

"This is fun." He bounced on his toes, looking around the room.

"Fun? This is not fun. It's capital punishment." Was he crazy? Suddenly, I noticed Coach Gray nearby, and the pieces fell into place. Denzel wasn't actually enjoying this.

He was just brown-nosing, trying to make himself look good by making the rest of us look bad.

Glancing over at Coach Gray, Denzel called out loudly, "Come on guys, pick it up. Let's go!"

"What the hell is Denzel doing?" James asked angrily, coming up beside me.

"Doesn't look like it's going to be pretty," I stated. Just then, Kadeem approached from the other side.

"This fool hasn't got our backs. He's selling us all out," Kadeem whispered, shaking his head in mistrust.

Noticing an opportunity, Coach Gray announced, "Denzel seems to be the only one in shape out here. If he wins another race tonight, you guys will run for the rest of practice."

Kadeem, James, and I exchanged glances. We were all beat; there was no way any of us could outrun Denzel, even if he had his eyes closed.

"Everyone on the line."

Making a point to stand next to Denzel, I leaned over to him and whispered, "The coach already knows you're in better shape than all of us, so hang back and let someone else win."

In response, Denzel grinned smugly, then got down in the starting position and prepared to take off. There was no way he was holding back. As soon as the whistle sounded, he was off the line and pelting down the court.

There was no way I was spending the entire second half of practice running. How could Denzel sign us all up for that without a glance back? Anger filled me, and my entire focus shifted to catching Denzel. Finding a deep-down reserve of energy I hadn't known was there, I sprinted after him until the two of us were head-to-head at the final stretch. Maybe he'd mustered some last-minute team spirit, or maybe he'd finally reached his limit, but in the last few steps before the line, Denzel slowed down, and I crossed a split second before him.

"Good job, Khalil," Coach Gray called.

Bent over and gasping, I waved a hand in his direction. I was just thankful Denzel had eased up.

After putting us all through a few shooting drills and a scrimmage match, Coach Gray whistled for everyone to come to the center of the court.

"Great practice, guys." Pacing slowly around all of

us, he took a deep breath, his face a bit downcast. "This is always the toughest part. You've all done great work today, but you know not everyone gets to stay. To those names I don't call, thanks for coming out, and maybe we'll see you again next year."

The first name he announced was Carson Maine, then Kevin Harding, starting center from the year before. Next came Kadeem, Denzel, James, and the other school recruits. We were down to the two walk-on openings. Despite my confidence in my skills, nerves twisted my gut. I held my breath.

Sweet relief swept through me as Coach Gray announced my name as the first of the two walk-on players. I smiled. I hadn't really been worried about not making it onto the team, but I was glad it was finally official.

# CHAPTER **17**

**Katrina and I were** in her dorm room, lounging on the bed and making out like our lives depended on it when Katrina's friend Angie Gordon stormed in.

"Your father is here!"

"What?" Katrina jumped out of bed, immediately grabbing a pair of sweats and hoodie out of the laundry bin. "Where? What the hell is he doing here?"

"I saw him outside. I don't know." Angie stood in front of the door like a bodyguard. "But if the two of you don't hurry your asses up and get dressed, we'll all be in trouble."

"What's the big deal?" I stared at the two of them, confused. I slipped on my basketball shorts and Haysville hoodie. "Your father knows about me, right?"

"Well, I haven't exactly told him," Katrina mumbled, then pivoted back to Angie. "What are we going to do?" she asked, wringing her hands.

"I got it!" Angie exclaimed. She reached up and wrapped her arms around my neck. "You will pretend to be my boyfriend instead, okay?"

"What? Why?" I tried to catch Katrina's eye, but she evaded my glance, stepping towards her desk instead. Quickly unwrapping and shoving three pieces of Doublemint gum into her mouth, she turned to the full-length mirror, chewing furiously while pulling at her clothing and trying to straighten her hair.

"Stop asking so many damn questions, Khalil," Angie slapped me in the back of the head. "Just follow my lead."

"No way. Why would I do that?" What the hell was going on here?

"Khalil," Katrina spun back to stare at me, tears in her eyes. "I'm begging you. Please pretend that you and

128

Angie are a couple. Please?"

The ghostly look in her eyes scared me. Against my better judgment, I agreed. "Okay, okay. I'll do it."

"Thank you, baby." She offered a small smile, then kissed me hard.

Moments later, the door opened.

Before her father could enter, Katrina dashed forward and leaped into his arms, forcing him back out into the hallway.

"What are you doing here?" she exclaimed. Peering over his shoulder, she mouthed "thank you" to Angie and me.

"So shocked," he chuckled. "Can't an old man surprise his baby girl?" Shaking his head, he turned and walked back into the room, Katrina trailing behind him. By now Angie and I were sitting at the desk in the corner of the room, pretending to be studying.

"You remember Angie, don't you, Daddy?"

"Of course, I remember, honey bee," he said to Katrina while cutting his eyes over to me. "How are you?" he said to Angie.

"I'm good," Angie smiled. "This is my boyfriend, Khalil."

"Nice to meet you, Khalil," he extended his hand, squeezing hard when I accepted.

"It's nice to meet you, too," I lied.

"So, where are you from, and how did you meet Angie and my honey bee?"

I glanced at Katrina, hoping for help, but her face was tight, her expression too guarded for me to glean guidance. Still, I couldn't leave the question hanging. I opened my mouth to reply, but before I could utter a word, Angie interrupted.

"Look at the time!" She waved her phone in the air. "I wish we could stay longer, but Khalil has basketball practice in twenty minutes, and I have to drive him. It was great seeing you again. Please don't be a stranger." She rose to her feet.

"So you're a ball player, huh?" Katrina's father asked, sizing me up as I stood to follow Angie out the door. "Have a great practice, and good luck this season."

"Thanks," I replied.

"That was a close one," she breathed as we rushed down the hall and out of the dormitory. "I'm parked right over here. Want a ride back to Lowell Hall?"

"Sure," I accepted. It wasn't that far of a walk, but I had questions, and it seemed like Angie had answers. "Thanks."

"No problem." She backed out of the spot and pulled onto the street.

"So," I dove right in, "what was that all about?"

"Are you kidding me?" She glanced over at me, her brows raised. "Khalil, you are too smart to be stupid. What do you think?"

"He's racist?"

"I wouldn't put it like that." She pulled into an empty parking spot in front of Lowell Hall. "Let's just say someone of our pigmentation will never mix with him or his kind. But listen - don't let it get to you, alright? Have a good night."

I climbed out of Angie's car with plenty on my mind. But I didn't have long to think about it. An hour and a half later, Katrina stopped by my dorm room to explain.

"Look, Khalil, my dad is an old-school Irish man. I'm sorry I have to hide our relationship from him, but it's the only way we can be together. He will never understand an interracial relationship, much less approve of one. I hope you can understand."

"Well, I don't understand. What does love have to do with color?" I retorted. I couldn't believe what I was hearing. It was just so stupid. Our relationship was forbidden fruit simply because the color of our skin was different.

Suddenly noticing the tears in her eyes, I tried to adjust my tone. Forbidden or not, Katrina and I were good together. I loved her and still wanted her, despite what her father thought.

"It's cool," I tried to laugh it off, ignoring the sick feeling lingering in my gut. "I get it. I don't agree, but I understand why you're keeping our relationship a secret."

"Thank you, baby," she smiled tearfully. Wrapping her arms around me, she kissed me, then pulled me down to lay on the bed beside her. Laying her head on my chest, she sighed and closed her eyes. Moments later, she was asleep.

# CHAPTER 18

**Haysville's first basketball** game of the season was less than a week away. The team was hanging out in the gym, waiting for the mandatory meeting Coach Gray had ordered. As soon as he walked in, dressed in a navy blue sweat suit, he called out.

"Get to center court! I've got an announcement to make." We all hustled to the center of the room. "After careful consideration," he continued, "I've selected our starting five."

There wasn't a player on the team who didn't want to

be part of this elite group. As a walk-on, the odds weren't in my favor, but I couldn't help but hope. I'd been on top of my game every practice since the day I'd made the cut. Starting would solidify my spot on this team, not to mention on campus, too.

"Who do you think made the starting team, man?" Kadeem immediately whispered to James, glancing my way but avoiding eye contact.

"I don't know, but I know it's not me," James replied.

"I'll tell you this, if I'm not on the starting team, then I'm quitting," announced Kadeem, still eyeing me.

*What's his deal?* I wondered. Did he see me as some kind of threat? We didn't even play the same position.

"You don't have to worry, man." Denzel told Kadeem. "You know you got your spot on lock." He was staring at me, too. Weird. I shrugged it off.

Coach Gray continued with his announcement. "At center will be Kevin. My power forward will be Martin, and my small forward will be Kadeem."

"Told you," Kadeem bragged to James.

"Now, the starting guards for this year's team."

134

Everyone held their breath. "Before I announce them, I want everyone to know that this year's team is the most athletically gifted team we've ever had. We have the potential to go all the way to the national tournament."

"Come on, Coach. Enough with this garbage speech. Just name the freaking starters," I whispered under my breath, maybe a little louder than intended. A few people glanced my way.

"We have a great group of guards this year, but the guard I'm most impressed with is a freshman out of Massachusetts, one who I believe has the ability to lead Haysville to a championship win this year, if he keeps his head together."

*It had to be Denzel,* I thought. He fit the bill, and we all knew Coach thought he was the best thing since sliced bread.

He continued, "This year's starting guards are Carson and our secret weapon." He paused and smiled, eyeing the team, then pivoted his eyes towards me. "Khalil, you will be our other starting guard."

Elated, I managed to keep my composure, though

excitement bubbled up inside me. A few feet away, Denzel dropped his head in disbelief.

"Congratulations to all our starters. I'd better see you all bring it in next week's game," Coach Gray concluded with a loud clap. Then he turned and hustled out of the gym.

# CHAPTER 19

The next day, I could barely keep my eyes open. I'd tossed and turned the night before thinking about the upcoming game. I managed to make it to my early morning class, business statistics, but as soon as I found my seat at the back of the classroom, I plopped down, propped my head on my hand, and closed my eyes.

"You okay, man?" Denzel asked, dropping into the seat next to me. As if to emphasize Denzel's words, Kadeem nudged me in the ribs from the other side.

"I'm beat, that's all."

"Well, this is your only class of the day. Just try to stay awake," Kadeem laughed.

Just then, Professor Barber stepped up to the podium and tapped the mic.

"Good morning, class. Today we'll be discussing a topic many of you may have never considered: race in consumerism. To start us off, I've got a question." He looked around the classroom. "Who do you think are the biggest consumers of lingerie, black women or white women, and why?"

He waited for an answer from the class, but no one volunteered. As if expecting this response, the professor smiled.

Looking to the back of the room, he asked, "Kadeem, what do you think?"

"I don't know."

"Does anyone want to answer this question?" Professor Barber asked a second time. Again, no one said a word. "Okay, since no one knows the answer, I'll tell you. The biggest consumers of lingerie are white women."

He grabbed a black marker from his desk and wrote

the words "black" and "white" on the whiteboard at the front of the room and circled the word "white."

"Can anyone think of why this may be so?" Again, no one responded. "I can see this is a touchy subject for some. Well, the facts tell us that white women buy more lingerie because they are not limited in what they can buy."

"What do you mean by that?" I blurted out, my tone a bit angrier than intended. *Blame that one on sleep deprivation.*

"Ah, so we do have someone who is willing to participate. Well, Mr. Gilliam," he smiled, "studies show that white women are more pleasing to the eye than black women when it comes to wearing lingerie."

He couldn't be serious. "Is this some kind of joke?" I responded, incredulous. "You're kidding, right?"

"Not at all. The statistics show that black women do not look good in the colors red, white, or pink."

"What? According to whom?" I asked. I was focused now, my earlier fatigue now vanished.

"Black women have darker pigmentation than white women, and thus, they are not as appealing as white women, especially in these colors," he stated calmly.

I looked over at Denzel and Kadeem for support, but they refused to meet my eyes. They stared forward, their expressions blank. Their lack of support incensed me almost as much as the professor's apparent inability to recognize the fallacy of his words.

There was no way I was going to let this slide. "Excuse me, Professor, but where do you get your facts?"

"I'm glad you asked," he said. "Everyone, open your textbook to page seventy-eight." Yanking my book out of my bag, I flipped quickly to the specified page. To my astonishment, there it was, in black and white: a whole chart of statistics comparing black women to white women. In a flash, my anger took over completely.

"Let me guess," I projected loudly. "The author of this book is a white man, right?"

At that, numerous heads whipped around to face me. Unaffected as they'd seemed up until this point, apparently this comment was enough to get my classmates engaged.

"We're just following what's in the book, Mr. Gilliam," Professor Barber assured me.

"Yeah, and slavery is in history books, too," I shot back, painfully aware of the stares of my mostly white classmates. There was no way I could back down now. "You know what's funny, Professor?"

"What's that, Mr. Gilliam?" His indulgent smile had been replaced by a deepening frown.

"This class is a joke. I was told we were here to learn about business statistics, but all I'm seeing is another example of how racist America really is. We claim equality, but as we've seen today, white people continue to degrade black people for reasons they cannot and will never be able to justify. Even today, in this class, racism rears its ugly head. Discrimination is apparently being taught as fact, simply because someone was racist enough to make a case study comparing the way black women and white women look in lingerie. Even worse, the school was racist enough to approve such a book!" I exclaimed, pausing to catch my breath.

With everyone still staring my way, I decided to go on the offensive. "Here's a better question for you, Professor: Why are white people afraid of black people?"

All eyes pivoted back to Professor Barber. "What makes you think white people are afraid of black people?" His tone was neutral.

"I think it's obvious, don't you? If they weren't afraid, I wouldn't be the only person in class debating with you about race. Why is everyone so afraid to speak up today? Every other day, the people in this class cannot stop talking, but today, no one other than me has said a single word. I mean, it's only a discussion stating white facts, right?"

The professor looked around the quiet room. "Does anyone want to address Mr. Gilliam's comments?"

The class was still silent.

"I told you," I said to Denzel and Kadeem.

"Enough, man," Denzel hissed under his breath.

"Anyone?" Professor Barber prompted again. "Will anyone speak to Mr. Gilliam's perspective?"

The longer the room remained silent, the more I felt like this couldn't be the end of the discussion already, not when there was so much still left to say.

"Last chance, folks. Does anyone have anything else to add to this discussion?"

"Yeah, I do," I spoke up again, still sounding as angry as I felt.

"We're all listening, Mr. Gilliam."

I took a deep breath and stood up.

"History books teach us that George Washington and Thomas Jefferson were great men and also our founding fathers," I began. "But what it doesn't teach us is that both of these so-called great men were slave owners. Thomas Jefferson stated, and I quote, 'Black people are one-eighth human.' These are the facts no one talks about, the things the history books gloss over.

"If we are going to discuss 'facts' in the future, let us discuss how racist America once was and unfortunately still is today. Let's remember how white people enslaved my people for over four hundred years. Let's talk about how, despite the abolishment of slavery in this country over a hundred and fifty years ago, discrimination and racism still run rampant today, barely beneath the surface. In today's society, racists are politicians, police officers, judges, lawyers, presidents, and even some of you sitting in this class. You know who you are.

"The problem is, no one is willing to talk about it. If I asked every white person in this room if they have ever used the word 'nigger' in their lifetime, which of you would tell the truth? Even if you might admit it to your white friends, you'd never admit it to me.

"Who are we fooling?" I threw my hands up. "I'm not racist, and I'm not promoting racism, but I'm sick and tired of white people trying to tell me about my race and define who I am. No disrespect to you, Professor Barber, but you should check your facts before you open up a class for discussion." I sat down.

By now, Kadeem and Denzel both had their backs turned to me, refusing to even look my way. But I didn't care. I'd done what needed to be done, even if it meant standing alone.

Seeing I had made my case, Professor Barber nodded, then looked around the room, trying to gather the class back together and wrap things up.

"Thank you, Mr. Gilliam, for enlightening us all. Class, your assignment for next time will be to read chapter six, and I want five hundred words from each of you on what type of business you think would be most profitable. Remember, I need to see facts. Class dismissed."

Reaching down to grab my bag, I stood back up to find Denzel right next to me. In a low voice, he said, "You are crazy, man."

"I'm crazy? Why am I the crazy one, Denzel?"

"Don't you know you can get kicked out of school for that stunt you just pulled?"

Kadeem came up beside him. "Yeah, man. What were you thinking? Have you lost your mind?"

I looked back at him. Did they not get it? I'd done what was needed.

"Nah, I haven't lost my mind, but I will tell you one thing." They were both staring at me. "I'm not and will never be a house nigger."

"What does that mean?" they asked in unison.

"It means I know my First Amendment rights, and I'm not selling my people out." Their jaws dropped. Brushing past them, I headed for the exit.

Before we could leave, Professor Barber interrupted us.

"A word, Mr. Gilliam." He pulled me to the side, allowing Denzel and Kadeem to pass. Figuring he was about to chew me out, I tensed up, awaiting his assault. But to my surprise, he clapped me on the shoulder, smiled at me, and said, "I just wanted to thank you for what you did today." Then he released my arm and walked away.

Dumbfounded, I stood motionless for a moment, watching his retreating back. Why had he thanked me? Now that the moment had passed, I wasn't so sure I'd made a difference at all. What had been gained? The whole lesson had been a complete waste of time. Shaking my head, I jogged out the door to catch up with Denzel and Kadeem.

# CHAPTER 20

**All of my hard work** in practice had paid off. I'd made the starting five. Now, it was time to prove I was the real deal, and my chance was imminent. Our first game in the fall basketball tournament was coming up, and we were scheduled to play our rivals, Winchester Technical College, who also happened to be last year's tournament champions.

The atmosphere was electrifying as we exited the team bus and confidently sauntered into the gym, looking every bit like a top collegiate program.

"You ready, KG?" Carson asked, coming up beside me. That was a surprise. It was the first time he had talked to me directly since tryouts.

"I'm ready."

"Okay, guys," Coach Gray gathered us together. "This is the first game of the season. Let's go out there, have some fun, and get revenge for our loss to these guys last year."

"Here's to an undefeated season," Kadeem cheered.

"And one last thing," Coach Gray looked at Denzel and me. "Carson will start the game running point. Khalil, you will start at shooting guard."

"Okay, Coach," Carson smiled. "I got this."

"I thought you were running point," Denzel whispered to me.

"Me too." I wasn't happy about Coach Gray's last-minute change. It would impact the whole team dynamic. More importantly, why did he think I couldn't handle it? I popped in my headphones and tried to tune out the pregame chatter of my teammates.

But a minute later, as we headed into the locker room,

Coach Gray pulled me to the side, motioning for me to pull out my earbuds. Hiding a sigh, I dutifully pulled them back out.

"I know you thought you would be starting at point guard, Khalil. But I believe Carson will be a better fit against this Winchester team. I'm confident this is the best decision for the team."

What was that supposed to mean? I didn't like the way his comment struck me, but there was no time to think about it. Moments later, we huddled up for Coach Gray's final pre-game instructions.

"Listen up. We're going to play a zone defense against Winchester because there's no way we can match them man-to-man." He looked at me. "But if the zone doesn't work, we'll have to give it a try. If we need to match up, Khalil, since you are our best defender, you will cover Rick Johnson. He's Tech's best player and their leading scorer."

I nodded.

"One last thing, guys," Coach Gray reminded, loosening his tie. "Do not try to run with this team, okay? Now, let's get out there."

We jogged out of the locker room and onto the court to begin warmups. Right out the gate, Kadeem wowed the crowd with his favorite flashy dunks. But our team's stunts didn't hold their attention for long. Moments later, loud music boomed through the speakers, and Winchester stormed out of their locker room and onto the court, decked out in flashy, blue-and-orange track suits with matching Nike sneakers.

It was hard not to compare: They looked like an NBA team, and we... Well, no one would mistake us that way. I could feel my teammates' energy plummet palpably. *Not good.*

Noticing our dreariness, Coach Gray herded us back into our locker room for another pep talk. I'd hoped for solid, encouraging inspiration to help us all get out of our heads, but he paced nervously in front of us, clutching his clipboard.

Finally, he seemed to realize we were all waiting on him. Turning to us, he blurted again, "Do not run with this team." Several of the guys glanced at each other. He'd already given those instructions. We needed more. But

Coach Gray just looked over at Carson and said, "Run the show, captain." Then he went back to his pacing.

With all eyes on him, Carson shrugged, then offered, "Let's head back out there to finish warming up."

*Is that it?* I wondered. It seemed pretty obvious the team needed more than that. But I'd already been demoted from the point, so I kept my mouth shut.

We exited the locker room to finish warm ups just in time to see several of Winchester's players perform a series of consecutive dunks. Unlike Kadeem, it was obvious their moves weren't for show. They were powerful, confident, and downright intimidating. I could see the fear in my teammates' eyes.

Glancing over at Carson, I waited for him to take the lead. But he appeared no more confident than the rest of the team.

Before we could really get going, the horn sounded. We all headed to our respective benches to prepare for battle.

Once more, Coach Gray stood in front of us. He had managed to stop pacing, but he looked more than concerned as he mumbled his instructions. "Okay, remember, don't run with this team."

*Again?* I raised my eyebrows. Behind me, a few murmurs arose. I wasn't the only one questioning his repeat directions.

"Great leadership, Coach," Kevin said under his breath, but loud enough that we all heard him.

Coach Gray called our starting five forward. Carson, Kadeem, Kevin, Martin, and I stepped out and headed for center court to meet Winchester's starting five. We all shook hands and took our places. Then the referee tossed up the ball for the tipoff.

In the first eight minutes, we had more turnovers than points. Despite his track record of success, even Carson struggled to get the ball over half court. One of Tech's guards kept putting on the pressure, staying right on top of him.

The lack of leadership and poor performance continued, and by halftime, we were down by twenty points. "Haysville sucks," heckled one of Winchester's players as we all jogged back to the locker room to regroup. I cringed. Winchester was definitely a good team, but so were we. Yet they were crushing us. It looked like we were putting in no effort whatsoever. It was embarrassing.

Moments later, Coach Gray stormed into the locker room.

"What the hell is going on out there?" He hurled his clipboard across the room and stood over Carson, nostrils flaring. "And you're supposed to be our leader?" He spun on his heel and marched back out of the locker room.

*So much for his support.*

"So, Captain," Denzel asked, looking at Carson. "What are we going to do now?" To my relief, Carson immediately stood up to address us.

"We're not out of it yet, guys. They are better than we are, but we still have twenty minutes to play. We know we're not going to win, so let's make it respectable."

My jaw dropped. *Respectable?* We were getting our doors blown off. I looked around the locker room. Heads were bowed and postures slumped. No one believed what Carson was saying. I was even more disappointed in *his* lack of leadership than Coach Gray's.

Something rose within me. I couldn't let the team go down like this, not in our first game. Someone had to step up, and it looked like it was going to have to be me.

"Listen," I stated loudly. "We may or may not win, but we can either walk out of this locker room with our heads down, or we can play the next twenty minutes as if our lives depended on it. We've all worked our butts off for the last two months to get ready for this. Winchester is good, but they are not twenty points better than we are. If we play as a team, we can come back. I even believe we can beat them." By this point I was standing.

"Denzel." His eyes snapped up to meet mine. I nodded at him. "Take the ball to the rack. No one can stop you from penetrating."

His eyes widened.

"Kadeem. Stop shooting off-balanced jump shots. Take the ball to the hole and dunk on those fools."

He shot me a short smirk.

"Kevin, your post-up moves are unstoppable. Why are you shooting three-pointers? Go to the hole, man."

"And Carson, roll off the high screens and start knocking down a few three-point shots."

He nodded in agreement.

Seeing I had everyone's attention, I continued. "The only reason we're behind so many points is because we allowed them to punk us out the gate. We let them get in our heads." I was really getting going now.

"But we are a better team than that. We're here to fight, and we came to win. Me? I plan to leave my shield out there on the battlefield. Who is with me?" I shouted. No one responded; the locker room was totally silent. Not waiting for them, I stormed out. I was ready, even if they weren't. But seconds later, the rest of the team came running out of the locking room behind me, fired up. I grinned. It seemed my speech had worked.

The horn sounded for the second half, and off we went. Unfortunately, it didn't take long to realize my speech had not had the positive impact I'd intended. If anything, we were playing even worse than we had in the first half.

*This is agonizing,* I thought. *So much for verbal leadership.* Figuring maybe there was still a chance to show instead of tell, I decided to take the game into my own hands.

"Let me run the point!" I tossed to Carson.

"But Coach said I'm running the point."

"Trust me," I said. Looking at me hard, he nodded. We huddled up at the break.

Carson spoke up. "KG is running the point for the rest of the half."

All eyes shifted to me. "Just follow my lead and we can win this game."

I scored the next ten points and we managed to trim the lead to twelve points. My jumpshot was on fire and for the first time all game, it looked as if we had a chance. The crowd was hyped and so were we.

Then it all tumbled down.

"Time out," Coach yelled to the referee. He was fuming. "What the hell is going on out there?"

"I thought it would be better if KG ran the point instead of me," Carson breathed heavily.

"Who named you the coach?" he spat his words. "Carson, you will run the point and KG will move back to shooting guard. Do I make myself clear?"

"Yes, sir," everyone shouted in unison. Five minutes later we were down twenty-seven points.

The final score was Winchester 75 - Haysville 45. Despite the loss, it had been an impressive first game for me. I'd led both teams in scoring with twenty-four points.

Rick Johnson and a few other ballers from Winchester headed my way after the final buzzer. "Excellent game, but your team sucks. You should think about transferring to Winchester next semester instead of wasting your time there."

"Yeah," I shrugged noncommittally.

The head coach of Winchester joined the conversation. "Good game, son. Too bad you didn't have any help out there." He handed me his business card. "Call me."

"Thanks." I accepted the card with a nod before heading back to the locker room. I had my academic scholarship to consider, so I doubted anything would come of his offer, but it was nice to be noticed for my skills, especially in the face of defeat.

# CHAPTER **21**

**A week later,** the team was on the bus headed back to Massachusetts, this time to battle an unknown school from Worcester. We'd barely pulled onto the interstate when Coach Gray passed out copies of a sheet of paper highlighting the top ten things he liked and did not like about our game against Winchester.

At the very top of the list, printed in bold capital letters for the whole team to see, he had written: **KHALIL IS NOT RUNNING THE SHOW.**

Denzel twisted around in the seat in front of me. "What does he mean you're not running the show?"

"I don't know what he means. Our team sucks anyways," I retorted angrily, though I knew it wasn't true.

Overhearing our conversation, Kadeem turned around. "Coach is tripping, man," he reassured me. "Don't sweat it."

"I'm not," I replied. But I was. I reached inside my wallet and pulled out the business card Winchester's head coach had handed me. "I should transfer to Winchester and make Coach Gray eat his words," I stated boldly. "This team sucks anyways," I repeated. A couple of angry glares had me eating my words. "No disrespect to you guys, Kadeem, Denzel, James," I backpedaled. The last thing I needed was for the team to be against me, too.

Playing it cool, I leaned back in my seat and stared out the window. But Coach's words cut deeply, and though I refused to let it show, on the inside, I fumed.

*I cannot believe he has the gall to pin our loss last time on me! Who is he to tell everyone I'm not running the show? And like this, afraid to even say it to my face. To hell with him,* I thought viciously. Grabbing my copy of his list from where it lay on the seat next to me, I crumpled it into a ball and threw it forwards, towards where Coach Gray sat. It fell short.

That night, we won by forty points. But I only scored five. The game after that, I scored just nine points. My poor performance didn't escape the notice of my teammates, but no one dared say anything. They didn't need to. I knew what the problem was. As much as I tried to shake it off, I couldn't help feeling I was someone else's scapegoat, and it was eating away at me.

Even off the court I wasn't myself. Katrina stopped by my room one night and laid me out.

"Baby, I gotta ask. What's going on with you? You started out as the top scorer, but Denzel said you've been checked out lately."

"Nothing is wrong," I defended. I knew he'd told her more than that, but I didn't really want to talk about it.

"Come on, I know there's something bothering you. Talk to me. Is it what the coach said about you?"

I remained silent, avoiding her gaze.

"Baby, listen to me." She grabbed my hand and stared into my eyes, her expression serious. "You're the best player on the team. Everyone on campus knows it. You can't let something as insignificant as a few words from the coach take you out. You are a leader, Khalil, and a natural-born one at that. I can see it, and so can your teammates. Let your skills and talent show the true leader that you are. You do not have to prove anything to anyone, especially some coach. Let go and let God."

"What does that mean?"

"It means it's clear that your gifts are from God. So, trust Him. Let Him use you to show the world how powerful He is through you. Alright? Now, get over here and kiss me already."

I acquiesced, but her words stayed with me after she left, leaving me awake and thinking long into the night. Katrina was right. I was a leader. Why should I back down? I would not take the back seat for anyone, especially a coach who couldn't appreciate my God-given abilities.

By the next game, I was back to my old self. I scored twenty points and had thirteen assists, leading our team to its third straight victory. It wasn't long before every newspaper in New Hampshire was talking about "Khalil Gilliam, Boy Wonder." No one on campus, even Coach Gray, could deny my superstar status. It had taken a serious mental shift, but finally, everything was going my way.

# CHAPTER 22

**The end of the first** semester was only a few days away, and most of campus was excited about heading home to visit loved ones over winter break. On my way back to my room one day, I overheard Denzel and Kadeem talking about their plans.

"I can't wait to see my girl," Kadeem said as I strode past the two of them unnoticed. "I'm going to blow her back out."

I chuckled to myself but kept moving. Almost no one I knew was thinking about sticking around campus over break, but I was seriously considering it. Given what I'd left behind at home, I wasn't sure I wanted to go back.

When I made it to my room, I decided to crash for a power nap before my next class. But before I could get settled, Katrina stopped by unexpectedly. The look on her face told me something was very wrong.

"We need to talk," she said, teary-eyed. "My father is taking me out of Haysville."

"What!? Why would he do that?"

"He says it has something to do with money," she sobbed, "but that's a lie. I think he knows about us."

"That can't be a reason to pull you out of school! Where will you go? What will you do? There has to be another way." I frantically paced the room.

"I don't know," she cried. "He's talking about transferring my credits to some community college near home. But maybe that's good news. Home is pretty close by. I will only be thirty minutes away from you, baby. Maybe I can come visit you on weekends or something," she said, looking down. Her words were hopeful, but her tone was not. We both knew the truth. The decision had been made for us. It was the end of our relationship.

That night, we made love for the first and only time. It was beautiful. I wished the moment would last forever.

The following week, Katrina was gone. With winter break around the corner, memories of Katrina everywhere, and no real reason to stick around, I decided to go home instead of staying on campus.

I'd been told Damien's car was once again in the shop, this time with a blown engine, so I purchased a Greyhound bus ticket to Boston. The trip was blessedly quick, with relatively few stops.

As soon as the driver pulled into the terminal, I disembarked, waiting impatiently for him to open the storage compartment and hand me my suitcase.

"Here you are, young man. Enjoy your visit." He plopped my bag on the ground at my feet.

Reaching down to grab it, I discovered the handle had broken off. I sighed. Weighing in at over fifty pounds, packed full of everything I'd thought I might need for an extended stay at home, getting the suitcase home without a handle was going to be a chore. Out of the corner of my eye, I spotted a taxi and quickly patted my pockets, looking for cash. But I came up with nothing but empty gum wrappers and lint. *So much for a taxi home.* Giving it one more try, I checked my inner jacket pocket. A dollar and eighty cents, just enough to take the subway.

Hauling my bag to the nearest subway stop, I managed to haul my bag onto the train. A short ride later, I hopped off at the stop closest to home. But I still had a twenty-minute walk, maneuvering my heavy suitcase with no handle. Sighing again, I gripped my suitcase as well as I could and trudged up the subway steps and out into the frigid, New England air. The cold wind ripped through my thin jacket, and I shivered hard. I kept going, though, intent on my goal, only stopping a few times to rest the extremely heavy suitcase. After what seemed like an eternity, I finally found myself standing in front of my family's building.

Realizing I didn't have my key on me, I rang the bell multiple times until Stephon finally flung the door open. A grin lit up his face, and he greeted me with a powerful punch to my chest. I tipped back, barely managing to keep my feet. I had completely forgotten about Stephon's regular punches and wanted to cry after the blow, but I was frozen to the bone and far too cold to complain, much less actually do anything. *Same old Stephon,* I told myself instead, stumbling inside. With Katrina gone, it had been a rough week topped off with a trip home from hell, and all I wanted was a mug of hot chocolate and a hug. Not unexpectedly, I got neither. No one even seemed to notice I'd arrived home. Come to think of it, where was everyone? Stephon was the only one I'd seen.

Trying to warm up, I rubbed my arms with both hands as I headed for the bedroom at the end of the hall. I swung open the door, then did a double-take. I didn't recognize the room at all. My belongings were gone, and it looked like Stephon had completely taken over. Even my bed was missing.

"Your clothes are in the living room closet," Stephon informed me casually from where he lounged on his bed. "Close the door on your way out."

I stood there in disbelief. Was I no longer a member of the family? Did they think Haysville was my permanent residence? Where was I supposed to sleep? Suddenly exhausted, I dragged my suitcase back down the hall to the living room and dropped down on the couch, resting my elbows on my knees and my head in my hands.

Just then, the front door flew open.

"What's up, Black Boy?" Damien blurted as he and the rest of my family trooped in, their arms full of grocery bags.

"Damien, I thought your car wasn't running," I reminded him angrily. "I had to walk home from the subway with a busted suitcase in this weather. I could have frozen to death."

"Shut up, Black Boy," he said in return, taking off his hat and coat.

After dropping the load of groceries in the kitchen, Mom came back into the living room and headed straight for me. She hugged me tightly and kissed my cheek repeatedly until I gently pushed her away. Ignoring Mom's onslaught, Dakota and Michelle peppered me with questions about what it was like at college, what kinds of things I'd done, whether the food was any good, and what I liked most and least. Meanwhile, Damien kept trying to interrupt loudly, asking whether I'd slept with any white girls yet.

Settling herself next to me on the couch, Mom took control of the conversation.

"So, baby, how has college been so far?" Everyone settled down, finding seats wherever they could.

"College is cool," I began. "I really like it. I'm the leading scorer on the basketball team." Stephon had joined us in the living room, and as I said this, he grinned. "I also made the Dean's list. And I met this girl I like."

At this, Damien leapt out of his seat and crossed the room, squishing himself down next to me on the sofa.

"She's a white girl, isn't she?" My whole family seemed to hold their breath. All eyes were on me.

"Yeah, she's white," I admitted.

I watched as the glint in Dakota's eyes dimmed. She looked aside. I could tell she did not approve. Michelle managed to plaster on a smile, but I could feel her displeasure, too. The two of them rose and headed for the kitchen. Glancing at Stephon, he met my eyes briefly, disappointment all over his face. Then he left the room, too, heading back down the hall. Only Damien kept talking, badgering me with questions about how good "the white girl" was in bed. I didn't respond; I just looked over at Mom, who still hadn't reacted to the news.

It was Mom's lack of comment that got me the most. The longer her silence dragged, the more I began to question my choice to tell my family the truth about Katrina's race. I loved Katrina, but my family's reactions made me wonder. Was I wrong for dating a white girl? By doing so, was I turning my back on my family and my race? With no answers, I decided to keep the rest of the story to myself. They didn't need to know my relationship with Katrina was over. It would only bring more questions.

Eventually Damien seemed to realize I was done providing details. He gave up and wandered out of the room. Mom, still silent, followed after him, leaving me in the living room alone with my thoughts.

Sadly, feeling alone like this, despite having my family around, was nothing new. Since I'd been away at school, it had been a while since I'd experienced it. But I hadn't forgotten, and feeling the same way again was no surprise.

What did surprise me was how long their silent treatment lasted over my announcement about Katrina. My whole family completely ignored me for the rest of the night, pretending like I wasn't even there.

The next morning, I woke early, largely due to the lumps and springs poking through the old couch that was now my bed. I hoped today would be better than the day before. The tension in the house after I had shared I was dating a white woman had been almost more than I could bear.

I rolled off the couch and headed for the kitchen. Grabbing some juice out of the fridge, I turned around to see Dakota standing in the kitchen doorway. I smiled at her in greeting, but as soon as she spotted me, she turned on her heel and stomped back down the hall without a word.

Sighing to myself, I returned the juice to its shelf and closed the refrigerator door. It looked like I was in for another day of being ignored.

# CHAPTER 23

I had only been home three days when I decided to go back to school early. The silent treatment had stopped, but it was obvious there wasn't room for me at home anymore, and I did not want to be a burden to anyone.

When I informed everyone of my decision, no one objected. Maybe they wanted me out. It didn't matter. Mom gave me some cash and kissed me on the cheek. Damien drove me to the subway station. The gestures were nice. They just felt like too little, and way too late.

I bought a one-way ticket back to Manchester. As I

boarded the bus and stared glumly out the window, I felt even more lost than I had before I'd come home.

I knew my family had my back, but they sure had a dysfunctional way of showing it. It hadn't been easy growing up with them. Then, before I had a chance to prove myself, I'd been shuttled off to the group home, then the juvenile detention center. I'd made it through relatively unscathed and had even earned my scholarship to Haysville. Then I met Katrina. Things had been going so well.

But now, with Katrina gone and no home to return to, I was having trouble seeing a way forward. Every thought of school and campus was filled with memories of her, and I kept dwelling on the times we'd shared. At least I still had basketball, but what was that worth on its own?

I stared at my downtrodden expression reflected in the bus window, barely recognizing myself. Once again, I found myself wondering who I even was.

# CHAPTER 24

**Denzel and I were** on our way back to Lowell Hall when an old Chevy Cavalier pulled up beside us, windows darkly tinted.

"Do you know them?" I asked Denzel.

"I don't," he shrugged.

Ignoring the vehicle, we kept walking. But the car moved with us, veering in to cut us off the road. Then, the front passenger window rolled down. Inside were two older white boys with full beards.

"Hey, niggers! Are you lost?" one of them called out.

He leaned out the window, pointed something at us, and, before I could register what was happening, sprayed the two of us with an onslaught of water from some kind of hose.

Reacting instantly, I whipped my bookbag off my shoulder and flung it towards the car, ready to take them down. I headed for the car with Denzel right behind me, but they sped off, shouting the word "niggers" repeatedly as they peeled out.

Denzel and I looked at each other, mirroring shocked expressions.

"What the hell was that?!" Denzel asked. Our clothes were drenched.

"Racism is what," I spat. "I can't believe stuff like this is still happening in America! Somebody's got to do something," I announced, my anger flaring. Being black in a primarily white school was bad enough, but this blatant act of racism was an impossible pill to swallow.

"What are you suggesting?" asked Denzel.

"I don't know, but we have to do something, man." I was agitated enough to knock out the first white person I saw.

Suddenly, it came to me. "I've got an idea."

"What's that?"

"Let's go to the Union Leader. Maybe they'll write a story in the newspaper to expose this racist city," I suggested. Denzel nodded his agreement.

Still dripping wet, we looked up the address. It turned out the office of the city's most popular newspaper was just a few blocks away. Walking in the door, an elderly white receptionist with ocean blue eyes greeted us.

"Can I help you?" She smiled kindly.

"We would like to speak to one of your reporters," I said directly.

"Yes, hold on, boys." She smashed a series of keys on the keypad in front of her and spoke briefly into the phone. Shortly thereafter, a tall, portly man with a noticeable bald spot came through a nearby wooden door.

"Hi, I'm Mr. Walker," he greeted us. "I'm the senior editor here at the Union Leader. What can I do for you boys?"

"I'm Khalil Gilliam and this is my friend Denzel."

"Khalil Gilliam?" He appeared pleasantly shocked.

"You're the standout point guard from Haysville College, right?"

"Yeah, that's me."

"You are a very talented ball player. How many points do you average per game now?"

"Twenty-two."

"Wow, that's great. Our newspaper loves you."

"That's cool, Mr. Walker, but we're not here to discuss basketball. Aren't you curious as to why our clothes are wet?"

"Why, yes. I did notice that. What gives?"

"Just a few minutes ago, Denzel and I were walking back to our dorm when two older white guys in a Chevy Cavalier cut us off, sprayed us with water, and called us niggers repeatedly. We're here to find out if you can write a story about the racism taking place here in Manchester."

Mr. Walker smiled indulgently. "I want to commend the two of you for your bravery, and I thank you for coming down here, but I'm afraid it's just not much of a story. Yes, racism exists in Manchester, but it's not really news. I'm sorry you boys had to experience this, but we have more important stories to report."

"Are you saying that racism is not important, Mr. Walker?"

"Look, son, we don't make the news. We just report what our viewers want to hear. As I said, racism exists. Welcome to America. You're just going to have to deal with it. But if you'd like to discuss your basketball performance, or you have some other worthy story, I'd be happy to listen." He looked at us both briefly, then retraced his steps back through the wooden door, leaving us alone and speechless.

Denzel and I exchanged a glance. The message we'd received was clear. As we exited the building and walked back towards campus, our clothes still damp, neither of us spoke. But I could feel the resentment building up inside, and the familiar flames of anger began to burn brighter. It wasn't just Mr. Walker's dismissive attitude about racism that got to me, though our whole conversation left a bitter taste in my mouth. Ever since I'd arrived at Haysville, I'd been plagued by racist comments, attitudes, and events. I'd been told that racist textbooks were "facts," forcing me to stand up for myself, and I'd had to deal with a basketball coach who, I'd finally concluded, refused to let me lead for no reason other than the color of my skin. Then there was Katrina... I didn't let myself dwell on that one too much. It was still too painful.

Instead, I focused on my anger. Thinking over everything I'd been through just because I happened to be born black incensed me. The more I reflected on it, the more my heart rate picked up. I could feel the deep, burning pulsing within.

America was supposed to be the land of the free and the home of the brave. Bravery took many forms. But freedom? I was still waiting to see. It seemed impossible when so much racism and hatred surrounded me.

Between my experiences with the white boys in the Chevy, Mr. Walker and his dismissive attitude, Coach Gray's ongoing bias, Katrina's father, Professor Barber and his "factual" textbook, and even all the schools that had rejected me based solely on my past, never giving me a chance, it was hard to deny what I'd read in a number of books in the detention center: White people really were all devils.

The second semester of my freshman year passed in a blur of practices, games, classes, and exams. I made it through, but I'd lost my earlier enthusiasm. Now everything felt heavy and dull. By the end of the school year, I could hardly wait to go home to see my family. Dysfunctional as they were, at least I knew who to be there.

# CHAPTER 25

**Sleeping on the living room** couch and storing my stuff in the community closet were the first signs that spending the summer at home would be much as I expected. My family mostly ignored me, except for the occasional punch from Stephon and ribbing from Damien. I made it through the three-month break, but by the time the end of summer rolled around, I was more than ready to go back to school. *Racists be damned.* I wasn't going to let them stop me.

As I entered my sophomore year, I threw myself into my schoolwork and basketball. Thoughts of Katrina derailed me at first, but as the weeks and months passed, the memories dimmed and became less distracting. Before I knew it, sophomore year was over, and I was headed back home again.

This time, I only made it a month before realizing I had to get out. The only highlight of my visit back home was reconnecting with Sanchez, who'd texted me out of the blue one night. We'd hung out a few times and had been texting on and off since. It was nice to have some kind of tie to my past other than my adoptive, dysfunctional family.

For my junior year, instead of sticking with the dorms again, Denzel, James, and I decided to get an apartment off campus. With no supervision and no limitations, we drank, smoked, and partied it up every weekend and often on weeknights, too. Reconnecting with Sanchez had reminded me of who I used to be, and as I fell further back in old habits, my grades started to slip. My academic scholarship was at risk, but the basketball honors continued to pile up for me. Before I knew it, I was named to the preseason All-American team. After that, I didn't worry too much about my grades. I figured I'd made myself pretty indispensable.

By the time senior year rolled around, I began receiving calls from professional basketball teams vying for my talent. I wanted to make it into the NBA, and I was quick to let anyone who seemed even the slightest bit interested know that I was going all the way.

I knew my skills would be on display for the recruiters during our championship game, so when the day arrived, I made sure to bring my best. Our opponents were fierce, and the score went back and forth for the entire first half. We'd managed to pull ahead again by two points when Denzel stole the ball and passed it to me. Confidently, I dribbled past the defender and spotted a clear path to dunk the ball. The crowd cheered me on as I went to jump, but before I could get air, I heard a loud pop and felt a hot sear of pain. I hit the gym floor hard. I quickly tried to stand, but my ankle screamed the moment I shifted positions. I crumpled back down on the wooden floor, gritting my teeth against the pain.

My teammates circled around me. "You're going to be okay," one of them said in a worried tone. Then the double doors of the gym opened up, and the EMTs rolled in a gurney. I closed my eyes, fearing the worst. They lifted me up and strapped my body down as the whole arena silently watched. I threw my arm over my face to hide my grimace of pain as they wheeled me out.

After they loaded me into an ambulance, we headed for Memorial Hospital. It didn't take long for them to discover I'd torn my Achilles tendon.

"I'm afraid it's unlikely you'll ever play again." I stared at the doctor as she shared my fate. Her tone was gentle, but I couldn't process her words. *No. This isn't happening,* I told myself. But it was. Just like that, my season was over, and so was my career.

I lay back against the hospital pillow and closed my eyes, waiting for the painkillers to kick in. In the midst of my pain, only one thing seemed clear: No one would want me now.

# CHAPTER **26**

**Following my injury,** Haysville lost every single remaining game of the season and finished last place in the division. Without basketball to take up my time, I managed to get my grades under control, but losing my ability to play weighed heavily on me. To numb the pain, I turned to partying.

I was lounging in the living room with Denzel, smoking a joint and watching the Celtics game, when my phone rang. It was a private number. I let it go to voicemail. Seconds later, it rang again. Same number.

"Are you going to answer that?" Denzel took a hit off the joint and passed it to me.

"Nope." I kicked my feet up on the table in front of me and inhaled. The phone rang again. This time, I answered. "Who the hell is this?"

"Who do you think it is?"

"Sanchez?"

"Yeah, boy. I'm at the front door. Open up."

I wondered briefly about the private number as I ended the call and leapt up, the joint still in my hand. I opened the door to see my old friend. "What are you doing here?"

"I'm here to watch my boy walk across that stage and get his college degree."

"I don't graduate until next week." I refrained from mentioning I'd made the decision not to attend the actual graduation ceremony. I'd thought about going, but everyone at school was excited about having their families watch them walk across the stage, and it seemed unlikely my family would show. Over the years, I'd played in over a hundred basketball games, and they'd never shown up, not to a single game. Time after time, I'd hoped to see their faces in the crowd only to be let down. I wasn't going through that again. When they'd arrived, I'd torn up and thrown out all the graduation invitations I'd been given. But Sanchez didn't need to know that.

I opened the door wider to let him in, suddenly noticing he wasn't alone. Recognizing the face behind him, I froze, then stepped forward angrily.

"What are you doing here, Leon?" I hadn't seen him in years, but I'd never forget the face of the punk who had landed me in the juvenile detention center.

"What's up, KG?" Leon replied coolly.

"What the hell is he doing here?" I glared at Sanchez. I was ready to knock a few teeth down Leon's throat.

"Chill, man. It's time to make peace with your past, KG." Sanchez sauntered into the living room with Leon following close behind.

"Tell me what this punk is doing here. Because of him, I spent way too much time in juvie," I gritted.

"Let it go, KG." Sanchez began to pop open the bottle of Dom Pérignon he'd been holding. "Leon is family and one of my soldiers. Right now, it's time to celebrate."

"One of your soldiers?" I was enraged. "The only

thing I'm celebrating tonight is your so-called 'soldier' getting his ass whipped."

"Lay off, KG. I promise, Leon had nothing to do with you going to juvie. It was that punk, Blake Harden."

"What the hell are you talking about?" I shouted. "I was there. Leon and that kid Blake testified against me in court that day."

"You're wrong," he said calmly. "Leon never testified against you. Blake did."

"Get the hell out of here." I'd held onto this injustice for too long. Leon had to pay.

"Okay, tough guy, whatever." Sanchez tipped the bottle back and gulped several times. "If it's revenge you want, then go for it--"

I spun on my heel to find Leon, who had wandered into the kitchen, so I could settle matters once and for all.

"--but you'll only be fighting your cousin."

His words stopped me in my tracks. "What the hell did you say?"

"Leon. He's your cousin. That's what I've been trying to tell you."

"You're kidding." My hands were now tight fists at

my sides. I was barely holding it together. "There is no way that snake is related to me."

"Listen, KG." Sanchez chugged some more champagne, then clapped me on the shoulder. "You are the only one of us to successfully make it out of the hood. Soon, you will have a college degree. I have plans for us, KG. Plans that will change our lives." He grinned.

I shook off his grip, ignoring his references to some grandiose plan. I was still prepared to fight. "Is it true, what you said? Are Leon and I really family?"

He nodded, tipping back the bottle once more.

"Damn." I slowly lowered my fists. "This is crazy."

Instead of a fight, I found myself with a new relative. I quickly learned Leon was no longer the kid he'd been at the group home. As he'd grown up, he'd changed his tune. Though I couldn't forget the incident that put me in juvie, I chose to forgive him. After all, he was family.

After swilling down the last of the champagne, Sanchez beckoned me over to the couch to fill me in on his plan: a proposed partnership after graduation. It would give us both the freedom, he insisted, to live the good life.

After everything I'd been through, I knew better than

to expect much from the white world. All my lofty college education had gotten me was a broken heart, a busted Achilles, and plenty of exposure to racist bigotry. Oh, and the opportunity to land a low-paying, nine-to-five in corporate America. *To hell with that,* I thought. A life of crime and drug peddling would at least be more lucrative. As Sanchez dove deeper into the details as to how we would use my degree to our advantage, I found myself nodding along. Sanchez had the master plan. All I had to do was execute it.

# CHAPTER 27

**Nipsey Hussle's "Racks in the Middle"** blared from the speakers, rattling the dance floor of Royale, Boston's hottest nightclub, as I strolled into the VIP lounge with a group of roughnecks. Dressed in all-black suits and looking every bit like the mafia, we were there to celebrate Sanchez's birthday.

It wasn't long before we were tossing back Bacardi shots and popping bottles of Dom Pérignon. As we partied, two beautiful ladies parted the velvet rope into the VIP lounge, apparently having slipped by the four-hundred-pound bouncer hired to keep the unknowns out.

"Who are they?" I nudged Sanchez, watching them from across the lounge. My eyes were locked on the brown-eyed cutie with the curly afro. She was rocking a sexy, black, cocktail dress that flowed gracefully over her ass, provocatively accentuating her luscious curves. She wore a rope necklace with a matching bracelet, telling me she was the contemporary urban type with a classy flair. Striking a pose, she paused and scanned the room, stopping when her eyes met mine. I held her gaze, willing her to come to me.

I'd never really been into any of the women that frequented the club scene. Most of them were either gold diggers or so-called Instagram models. This girl was gorgeous enough to be all over social media, but I had a feeling she wasn't. There was something different about her.

"You feeling shorty, KG?" asked Sanchez with a grin, noticing my silence and my stare.

"Maybe," I tossed back nonchalantly, intentionally shifting my eyes away. But I found myself searching her out again immediately, pleased to discover she and her friend were approaching us.

"Ladies," he stood as they walked up, "my name is Sanchez, and this is my boy, Khalil." At six foot three with movie-star good looks, Sanchez carried himself with the confidence and swag of a professional athlete. "Join us. Drinks are on the house!"

"Hi," clamored the taller of the two enthusiastically. She was also a beauty, with alluring hazel eyes, short hair, and flawless bronze skin. Her perfect white teeth flashed as she did a subtle wave, acknowledging our group. "It's nice to meet all of you. I'm Cynthia, and this is my BFF, Nicole."

"Likewise," Sanchez replied. His focus was on Cynthia, but I still couldn't take my eyes off Nicole.

"Take a picture," Nicole smiled at me. A tiny dimple appeared near the corner of her mouth. "It may last longer than that stare of yours." She offered a flirty wink.

Her comment caught me off guard. To collect myself, I reached into my pocket and quickly withdrew my iPhone.

"Say cheese," I instructed cheekily. She struck a

playful pose, adding a naughty smile that almost threw me off my game again. I quickly snapped the picture.

"I like a man who is quick on his feet." Between her well-timed comments and suggestive smiles, I soon discovered conversation flowed easily with Nicole. As we talked, my eyes never left her, though I noticed she occasionally glanced across the lounge to the bar where Sanchez and Cynthia were hanging out, chatting and drinking away.

"So, Khalil," Nicole inched closer, leaning in and offering me a tempting glance down the front of her scoop-necked dress. "What is it that you do for a living?"

*What? Where had that come from?* Business was the last thing I wanted to be talking about. I leaned around her to grab another Bacardi shot from the table and quickly knocked it back.

"With all due respect," I replied, grabbing another shot and gulping it down like the first, "I'm a private person, and I'm very careful about what I disclose. No disrespect." I peered over at the bar where Sanchez was now twirling Cynthia as if she were a ballerina.

Nicole raised her eyebrow at my reaction but let it go. "None taken," she said lightly. I relaxed a little, looking back at her again. She matched my gaze, curiosity now mixing with the lust and intoxication I'd see in them all night.

As the silence dragged, I began to feel uncomfortable.

"Give me your phone," she suddenly said, extending her arm and flashing a grin. "And don't forget to unlock it, either."

I hesitated.

"Come on and hand it over," she pressed.

I reluctantly released my unlocked iPhone. Before I knew what was happening, Nicole maneuvered herself into my lap, leaned back, and snapped a selfie with both of us in it.

Laughing out loud, she turned the phone towards me. "Don't we look good together?" I nodded, acutely aware of her curves pressed up against me.

*What is it about this woman?* I didn't know whether I was mad or just mesmerized, but I kept wondering whether she tasted as good as she looked. I wanted to find out. I was ready to unleash the magnetism we both felt.

"Here's my number." Slipping off my lap, she scribbled on a napkin, then handed it to me with my phone.

Slipping the number in my pants pocket, I opened my phone and stared at the picture. She was right; we really did look good together.

Placing her hand on my arm, Nicole turned to me once more and smiled. "I think I'm going to call it a night." With drinks on the house, she grabbed a bottle of champagne from the table, then headed to the bar where Cynthia and Sanchez had just tossed back another round of shots. Nicole whispered in Cynthia's ear, and Cynthia nodded and held up one finger. Nicole headed for the exit.

Before following her friend, Cynthia whipped around and kissed Sanchez hard. "Call me." She grinned, then ran after Nicole.

"This was the best night ever," Sanchez sighed as he watched her go, weaving slightly where he stood. Then he slapped me on the back of the neck. "You are my man, fifty grand."

"You're drunk," I laughed, pushing him ahead of me and out the door. As Sanchez stumbled out, he started shadow boxing the air. He was known to get violent when he knocked back one too many, and this looked like the start. Better to get him home now. I found the limo driver parked out front. He opened the door as we approached and helped me wrestle Sanchez into the back seat.

"Get him back to the hotel in one piece," I requested. I slid the driver a hundred-dollar bill. Seconds later, they were gone.

Feeling a little tipsy myself, I strolled back inside the club to round up the rest of the crew when I spotted Nicole yelling at the bouncer from the VIP section.

"What's going on?" I stepped in. "I thought you left earlier." I looked at Nicole.

"Cynthia came back in," she shouted, waving her hands in the air. "And now fatboy here won't let me in to find her. I bet if I was holding a bucket of Popeyes chicken, his fat butt would let me in."

"Not without some Texas Pete," he shot back.

"Just let her in," I laughed. His Texas Pete comment was pretty funny.

"Yeah, let me in, you Biggie Smalls wannabe," she punted.

"Anything for you, KG," he nodded, unhooking the chain and waving us in.

Nicole and I searched the club for Cynthia, but there was no sign of her. Suddenly, Nicole's cell phone rang. As she looked down, Cynthia's name flashed across the screen, and Nicole's body relaxed.

"Where the hell are you?" she screamed into the phone, looking around for the exit. Spotting it, she turned to face me and asked, "Can you give me a couple of minutes?" I nodded, and she began to weave her way through the crowd towards the red exit sign.

I headed back into the VIP room, where the crew was still partying like there was no tomorrow. I waved at those whose eyes caught mine. The minutes seemed to drag, though. Had Nicole found Cynthia? I headed for the exit, too. Maybe I could find her. But before I could slip out, Cynthia appeared in front of me.

"Have you seen Nicole?"

"She walked out of the club a few minutes ago looking for you," I said, confused. "Weren't you just on the phone with her?"

"She told me to meet her back here."

The feeling I'd had earlier suddenly intensified.

Something was wrong. "I'll be right back." I dashed out the exit to find Nicole. Which way would she go? Before I could decide, I heard a loud scream.

"*HELP!*"

Something was wrong. "I'll be right back," I dashed out the exit to find Nicole. Which way would she go? Before I could decide, I heard a loud scream.

"HELP!"

# CHAPTER **28**

**I rushed towards the** sound. "Nicole?" I called out. "Where are you?" Frantically, I looked around. Then I spotted her, lying on the cold concrete, curled up in the fetal position.

"Are you okay?" I queried gently as I reached her side. My voice was strangely soft considering how ready I was to cause bodily harm to whomever had hurt her.

Finally, she met my eyes. Her lip trembled, and a fresh set of tears overflowed. "They stole my car!"

"Who stole your car?"

"Two guys wearing black ski masks came up behind me, threw me down, and stole my brand-new Mercedes Benz."

I helped her to her feet, and she clung to me for a moment. Then, reaching up, she wrapped her arms around my neck, pulled me down, and kissed me softly on the cheek.

"What was that for?" I asked, looking down at her. Even with tears tracking down her face, she was gorgeous. I knew it wasn't the moment to take things further, but I found myself hoping for more anyways.

"For showing up when I was alone." She leaned against my side, resting her head on my chest for a heartbeat before pulling away.

"Which way did they go?" I asked, leading her safely back inside the club.

"I don't know." She wiped away the tears with the back of her hand. "I need to call the police."

When the police arrived, Nicole filed a formal report about the attack and stolen car.

"Two men in black ski masks doesn't give us much to go on," one of the officers cautioned. "Don't hold your breath." Handing her a copy of the report, the two men left the club. I wondered if they'd even try to find the car.

With Nicole still clinging to me, I called the limo driver to pick us up. *He should have dropped Sanchez off by now,* I thought, but it seemed to take him forever to arrive. When he finally pulled up, I opened the rear door and ushered Nicole inside.

"Apologies for the delay."

"Where is Sanchez?"

"Back at the hotel with a woman he had me circle back to pick up," the driver confirmed.

"What did she look like?" I asked.

"She was a slender woman with short hair and light-colored eyes." He pulled away from the curb. "Quite striking," he added. Staring in the rearview mirror at us, he slowed down as he approached the intersection. "Oh, and she was wearing a black dress."

"Was it her?" Nicole reached through the partition, holding her phone out with a picture of Cynthia for the driver to see.

"Yes, that's her."

I rolled my eyes. Of course. *That was Sanchez for you.*

Relieved, Nicole sat back down next to me and rested her head on my shoulder.

"Where to?" the driver asked, glancing at us in the rearview a second time.

Nicole was silent for a long time. Finally, she lifted her head and spoke. "Home, please." She quickly rattled off the address.

"Of course." As the driver rolled up the partition window, she rested her head back on my shoulder and closed her eyes. Seconds later, she was asleep. I couldn't blame her. It had been one hell of a night.

# CHAPTER 29

**Sanchez called me early** the next morning bragging about adding another notch to his belt. "She did things to me that I never knew existed, man!" he exclaimed, shouting into the phone.

I pulled the phone away from my ear and flipped it to speakerphone to preserve my eardrums. "Is that so?" I asked nonchalantly, scrolling through a few text messages, not really listening.

"She may be the one. She has the potential to be my future wife."

"That's cool," I replied distractedly. I was trying to find Nicole's number, but I'd scrolled through my entire contacts list with no luck. I knew I'd gotten it from her. She'd had my phone. I had a picture of us together. Surely she'd put her number in there somewhere. Where could it be?

"Are you listening to me, KG?"

"Yeah, I heard you. She could be the one. How many times have I heard that before?" I needed Nicole's number, not to hear about Sanchez's latest conquest. Suddenly, I recalled she'd jotted her number on a napkin... that I'd stupidly tossed out when I'd drunkenly emptied my pockets into the trash can outside my building the previous night. I'd then stumbled into my apartment and straight to bed.

*Damn. How could I be so dumb?* Frustration mounting, I cut Sanchez off. "I gotta go." I ended the call before he could respond.

Sitting on the edge of my bed, I held the phone in my hands and stared at the screen for a minute, willing Nicole's number to somehow appear. Finally, I gave up.

Tossing the phone on my bed, I quickly undressed and headed for the shower. *I guess it wasn't meant to be,* I told myself. My gut twisted at the thought.

For the rest of the day, I tried not to think about Nicole. But thoughts of her lingered all day. Later that evening while I was chilling on the couch and watching the Celtics game, Sanchez called again.

"What's up?" I was not in the mood for idle chit-chat.

"The Royale is off the hook," he said excitedly. "Get dressed and meet me here. I promise you will thank me later."

I considered it for a moment. If my headspace was any indication, a distraction was probably a good idea. Trying to muster some enthusiasm, I agreed.

Sanchez was chatting with the owner of the club just outside the entrance when I arrived. He was all smiles. "Tonight is our lucky night." He grabbed the back of my arm and led me inside.

"What happened to what's-her-name from last night being the one?"

"I was tripping, man," he laughed. "I'm too much man for just one woman."

Walking in the door, it was obvious Sanchez was right. The club was jam-packed with women. Rather than feeling excited at the prospect, though, I found myself hoping I might run into Nicole again.

As soon as we set foot inside the VIP room, Sanchez grabbed a bottle of Hennessy from the bar and headed back out to the dance floor. "It's on," he said. "You coming, KG?"

"Nah, not yet. I'll catch up with you." I knocked back a couple of shots, but after a few minutes, I decided to call it a night. All I could think about was Nicole; the last thing I wanted was a drunken midnight rendezvous with some stranger. *If only I hadn't thrown out her number,* I berated myself, grabbing my keys from the pocket of my jacket as I headed out.

# CHAPTER 30

**The next day**, I received another call from an unknown number. I let it go to voicemail, but I found myself frowning. I didn't like how many calls I'd been getting lately from people I didn't know. Besides me, Sanchez was the only other person who had my number, and I preferred it that way. *Maybe it's time for a new number,* I mused. Moments later, my phone buzzed again, indicating a voicemail.

"Hey, KG. It's Henry Banks. Meet me at Johnson Brothers warehouse in one hour. Call me as soon as you get this message."

*Weird call,* I thought as I listened to his hasty voicemail.

Henry Banks was a local drug-dealing crackhead from Somerville, a mostly white neighborhood on the outskirts of Boston. Curious, I retrieved a spare burner phone from the glove compartment and dialed.

"What's going on?" I said with an attitude. "And how did you get my personal cell number?"

"I need you to meet me at the warehouse in an hour. I have a surprise for you."

"I hate surprises."

"Well, you will like this one," he laughed.

I pulled into the Dunkin' Donuts parking lot for my morning coffee. "Enough BS. What's the surprise?" I was tired of the games.

"Trust me," he laughed a second time. "You are the last person on earth I would ever betray. On my life. Just be there. You won't regret it, promise. See you soon, KG."

Mashing the button to end the call, I tossed the burner back into the glove box. Thinking for a moment, I decided to call Sanchez. Maybe he knew something I didn't.

"What's up KG?" he answered groggily.

"Tell me you're not still in bed. It's 11:30 AM."

"How I spend my days is my business," he shot back. "And you know how I like to spend my nights. Besides, I'm over here sinning with a woman who is capable of taking me off the market."

"That one from the club before?"

"Nah. She's old news. I traded her in for a Gabrielle Union look-alike."

"Damn," I shook my head. "Please make sure you are protecting yourself."

"Come on, KG. Condoms are like my American Express card. I never leave home without them," he laughed. "So, what gives? Why the early morning call?"

"You remember Henry Banks?"

"Yeah. What's up?"

"He just hit me up on my personal phone and asked me to meet him at Johnson Brothers warehouse."

"Did he say why?"

"No. You wouldn't know how he happened to have my number, would you?"

"Sure. He called me the other day, and I gave it to him."

"Why would you do that?" I gritted.

"Just meet him, then call me after."

"What? Why? What the hell is going on, Sanchez?"

"Do you trust me?"

"With my life," I responded automatically, feeling a little annoyed.

"Well, meet him."

"Fine." Whatever Sanchez's deal was, I wasn't getting any more details. It looked like I was headed out to meet Henry Banks.

"Peace, KG."

"Peace." I ended the call. Moments later, I turned onto Interstate 93.

# CHAPTER 31

**It was 11:48 AM** when I arrived at the Johnson Brothers warehouse. Still feeling unsure about meeting someone I definitely didn't trust, I lifted my nine-millimeter from the glove compartment and loaded the clip. Taking a deep breath, I exited the vehicle, praying I wouldn't shoot some unexpecting, unarmed person. There was already plenty of that going around without my help.

Channeling my old days of being the school bully, I strutted towards the warehouse fearlessly. I was ready to put a hollow-point bullet in anyone who had the courage to threaten me. I even slapped on a nonchalant expression for good measure, though I hadn't seen anyone around yet. Whoever was there, I wanted them to know I was ready for whatever might be coming my way.

Reaching the door, I pulled hard on the old, rusty handle. The heavy warehouse door swung open smoothly and quietly, surprising me. I'd expected rusty, screeching hinges. As I entered the dark and shadowy warehouse, I raised my guard and my gun higher. Anything or anyone could be hiding inside.

Keeping my footsteps quiet, I silently searched amongst old machinery and long-abandoned barrels, but I found no one. As I silently cleared the far end of the warehouse, the warehouse door swung open again, bathing the room in bright light. Footsteps smacked the cement floor. Ducking behind a nearby column, I held my breath. *That better be Henry.* I rested my finger on the trigger of my gun. Before I could move, I heard a second set of footsteps echoing through the warehouse.

Henry obviously hadn't come alone. Realizing I'd been set up, my anger spiked, sending adrenaline coursing through my veins. *How dare that scum try to pull one over on me,* I thought murderously. Who does he think he is? I sucked in a deep breath. I didn't know what was coming, but if this went down, somebody could die. I was going to make damn sure it wasn't me. *I'm going to have Sanchez's head for this,* I fumed silently. This is exactly why I don't share my number.

I waited in the shadows as the first set of footsteps drew closer. With the element of surprise on my side, I leaped from behind the column and cracked the traitor across the face with the back of my gun. He crumpled without a sound, dropping to the floor. It took only a few seconds before blood began to pool under his head. Nudging him with my foot, I managed to roll him over onto his back. It was Henry.

"Didn't I tell you what would happen if you betrayed me, you punk?" I hissed at his unconscious face. Just then, a voice rang out.

"Henry? Where are you?"

I stepped quickly into my hiding spot before the second ambusher spotted me. Moments later, a well-dressed man appeared. He rushed towards Henry.

"Who did this to you?" he demanded urgently, grabbing Henry's shoulders and shaking him. His focus was entirely on the bleeding man. Quietly, I stepped out of my hiding spot and approached him from behind.

"It was me." I pressed the cold steel of my nine-millimeter against the back of his head. He froze.

"Don't shoot," he begged.

"Who the hell are you?" I demanded.

"My name is Todd Banks," he rushed out. "I'm here because--"

"Turn around slowly." Stepping back, I locked a bullet into the chamber, my aim steady. Slowly, he spun around to face me.

"I'm your twin brother," he finished quietly, lifting his eyes to meet mine.

I managed to hold the gun steady, but only barely. What kind of comment was that? Was this some kind of twisted joke? I didn't have a twin. Who was this guy? Using the shadows to my advantage, I looked him over.

The more I looked, the less I could believe my eyes.

He was a stranger, but the resemblance between us was astonishing.

"Listen," he pleaded, interrupting my silent musing. "I found out about you at our father's funeral. Until that moment, I didn't know you existed. I came today to find out the truth."

This was too much. A dead father on top of a twin brother? Did I have other family members I didn't know about, too? Siblings? Cousins? Nieces or nephews? Were they alive? Did anyone else know about me? Were they also looking for me? If they were, why had they given me up all those years ago? And why me, not *him*? I couldn't shake the surreal feeling that I was in a movie, only instead of watching, I was the main character.

But there was no way I was going to open up to some random stalker I didn't even know, even if we did share the same face.

"You shouldn't be here," I finally barked. "There are some things that should stay buried." The more my thoughts churned inside me, ricocheting around with nowhere to go, the angrier I could feel myself becoming.

"Even if we are brothers," I continued, my tone venomous, "the world I live in is far from the bourgeois life you clearly live."

Keeping my gun carefully trained on him, I began to circle around slowly, maneuvering my way towards the exit. A quick glance at the floor told me Henry was still out cold. Before I slipped out the door, I decided to drop a few final words of wisdom.

"My advice to you, *brother*, is to stay the hell away from me... Otherwise, you may find yourself eulogized." Two steps later, I was out the door and headed for my car.

# CHAPTER 32

**Slamming the door shut,** I floored it, peeling out before turning towards the interstate. *This cannot be real. This cannot be real. This cannot be real,* I chanted to myself as I took the on-ramp at nearly fifty miles an hour. I zipped in and out of highway traffic, trying to shove down my tumultuous emotions.

Finally, I couldn't take it anymore. I grabbed my phone from the console and called Sanchez. Four rings later, he picked up.

"What's up, KG?" His voice was lethargic.

"You do know it's not normal for a healthy man your age to sleep his life away, right?"

"How I choose to live my life is my business, KG." His tone was cold. I'd apparently struck a nerve. "Besides, I'm a night owl," he reminded me, his tone lighter this time.

"Fact," I laughed. "But that's not why I'm calling. You will never guess what just happened to me."

"Well, don't keep a brother in suspense."

"I think I met my twin brother today."

"What?" He sounded genuinely surprised. "When Henry asked for your number, he told me he found your brother, but he never mentioned it was your *twin* brother. That's crazy."

"Sanchez, how long have we known one another?" I demanded.

"Fourteen years. Why do you ask?"

"Because after all this time, I thought your loyalty was to me, not a freaking crackhead. You should've told me the minute he contacted you. We're boys."

"Lighten up, KG." I could practically hear him roll his eyes. "Stop whining like a baby. Henry asked me not to let onto the surprise, and it sounded like a good one, so I kept my mouth shut. Turns out it was an even better surprise than I thought. A twin, huh? Separated at birth? That is crazy. It's straight out of a soap opera.

"Anyways," he continued without waiting for my response, "the truth is out now. So… what are you going to do?"

*Just like Sanchez.* Leaving me in the dark for the sake of some stupid surprise. I was pissed, but I also knew he was right. For better or worse, the truth was out. I just didn't know what my next move was.

"I don't know, man. What do you do when you're confronted with the long-lost twin you never knew you had?"

"Well, you can start by getting off of the phone with me and calling him."

"Um… I can't."

"Damn, KG," he grunted. "Please tell me if the two of you at least exchanged phone numbers."

"In my haste, I might've told him to stay out of my life."

"You know, you really have to do something about that temper of yours. Do you at least know his name?"

"Yeah. His name is Todd. *Todd Banks.*"

# CHAPTER 33

"Do you remember that fine girl I met at the club?" Sanchez asked, changing gears on me mid-stride.

I rolled my eyes. Sanchez had more women than King Solomon. There was no way I could keep up.

I put him on speaker phone. "I need more details."

"The dark-skinned one that slapped me on the ass in front of the crew during my birthday bash? The one that looked like Naomi Campbell?"

"I wouldn't go that far," I laughed. "But, yeah, I remember. She's friends with Nicole, right?" *The one I'd let get away.* I shook my head. I still couldn't believe I'd made the rookie mistake of inadvertently tossing her number in the trash, even if it had been an eventful night.

"Sure, whatever." Sanchez's comment brought me back to the present. He lowered his voice, whispering into the phone. "She's in my bathroom taking a shower right now."

"Really?" I matched his whisper.

"Wait, why are *you* whispering?" he asked, his volume normal.

"No idea." I spoke normally this time, too. We both laughed.

"Anyways, what I'm trying to say is Henry isn't the only one full of surprises today. Guess what?"

"I'm listening."

"This sexy thing is also the VP at Verizon."

"Yeah?"

"She is fine, sexy, and successful. And, let me just tell you, she knows her way around the bedroom. The things this woman can do with her mouth and tongue would have your head spinning."

"TMI, man. That is way too much information."

"Don't hate, KG," he laughed. "After another sexathon with what's-her-name, I'll have her hunt down your *twin* brother's contact information."

"If you're not too distracted by *what's-her-name,* ask her for Nicole's number for me, too. She may have moves, but Nicole and I have a lot of catching up to do... if you know what I mean."

"I got you, man."

"Peace, Sanchez."

"Peace, KG."

Ending the call, I tossed the phone on the seat next to me. I hoped Sanchez would come through with Nicole's number, but I needed a coffee. Spotting a Dunkin' Donuts ahead, I pulled into the parking lot. I'd no more than turned off the engine when my phone dinged with a voice memo from Sanchez. That was quick. I tapped the message to play it.

"Good news, KG," Sanchez's voice greeted me. "I managed to kill two birds with one stone. You'll be happy to hear Cynthia's friend Nicole has also been looking for you. I'll text you her contact info. Also, I managed to find out more about your brother. I hope you're sitting down for this one because... well, let's just say he grew up on the other side of the tracks. Your so-called brother is a well-known Boston attorney. I looked him up, and you were right, he is definitely your twin. A better-looking version of you... ha! I'm sending you two numbers, his cell phone and his office. But before you contact him, a word to the wise, KG. Some things should remain buried... Be careful. Love you, man. Peace!"

I sat there for a moment after the message ended and silence filled the car. *An attorney,* I thought. *How ironic. If only he knew the kinds of things I was up to.* My mother had always preached that my worst enemies would be members of my own family. Well, now I had a long-lost twin brother who could be the very person to take me down. Looked like I hadn't given Mom nearly enough credit.

Grabbing Nicole's cell and the two numbers for Todd from Sanchez's texts, I locked them into my contact list. I wasn't sure what I was going to do about Todd, especially after Sanchez's ominous and unsolicited warning about keeping things buried, but Nicole was another story. I knew just what I wanted to do with her number... and with her. Smiling to myself, I climbed out of the car and headed inside for my coffee.

I was standing in line with a few customers ahead of me when my phone dinged again. I tapped the screen to unlock it and discovered a new text message. It was Nicole.

*Hey stranger... My girl Cynthia gave me your number. She told me you were looking for me. I thought you ghosted me after saving me that night, but I'm going to give you a pass and blame it on the alcohol. You have two more strikes... LOL. Let's meet up for coffee sometime. Side note: I like my coffee strong and black. Ciao. :)*

Grinning, I tapped the screen and began my reply.

"May I take your order?" interrupted an attractive Latina with shoulder-length, wavy hair.

Realizing there were no longer any other customers in front of me, I stepped forward and glanced at the menu, trying to decide whether I wanted something more with my coffee. "Let's see. I'll start with a medium hot coffee with one cream and two sugars."

"Got it. Will that complete your order?" She leaned forward and smiled, showing cute dimples in both cheeks.

"No. He will also have a large black coffee with no cream, no sugar." I knew that voice. I just needed to see her face to confirm. I spun around, and there she was, looking as beautiful as I remembered.

"Nicole!"

# CHAPTER 34

**"So, *KG*,"** she began, her tone flirty. "That's what your friends call you, right?"

"Only my friends," I laughed. "But *you*, you can call me Khalil."

"Good," she replied, looking me up and down. "I have never been an acronym kind of girl, anyway. Khalil will do better."

Just then, the barista cleared her throat loudly. "One medium coffee with cream and two sugars for the gentleman, and a strong, black coffee for you." Her dimples had disappeared.

"Here." I handed her a hundred-dollar bill. "Keep the change."

"Gracias, guapo," she said enthusiastically, her smile returning. Slipping the tip into her back pocket, she grabbed a napkin, jotted something on it, and handed it to me with a wink. "Llamarme."

"If you don't take your Goya-bean-eating ass to the back and make some donuts..." Nicole interjected stormily. Staring at the barista, she grabbed the napkin from me and shredded it into pieces.

Noticing we were on the verge of a heated altercation, I decided it was time to go. Grabbing her by the shoulders, I ushered Nicole out the door, leaving our coffees on the counter.

"Can you believe that trick, acting as if I were invisible!" she fumed. "I should have slapped the taco meat out of her."

I raised my eyebrows. "You know that's racist, right?"

"Well, they do eat tacos!" she retorted.

Laughing, I shook my head. "You are trouble."

"The worst kind of trouble for a man like you," she grinned.

"I like where you're going, but hold that thought for just a second." I dashed back inside to retrieve our coffees. When I came back out, Nicole was standing next to a two-door, black Mercedes parked a few spots down from me.

"Strong and black, just the way you like it." I handed her the cup.

"Thank you, Mr. Gilliam."

"It's the least I can do for a woman as beautiful and feisty as you."

Taking the cup, she leaned back on the hood. "So, big spender, I heard a big secret was revealed to you today."

I nearly choked on my coffee.

"Where did you hear that?" I asked, trying to sound casual. *Damn Sanchez and his pillow talk.* No doubt Cynthia had filled her in.

"If I tell you, I may have to kill you. And that wouldn't be fun." She stepped closer, wrapping her arms around my neck. Instantly I became aware of her body pressed close against mine.

Wrapping an arm around her waist, I pulled her closer.

She looked up at me with a knowing smile. "You want me, don't you, KG?" she purred.

"Yeah," I replied gruffly.

Holding my eyes for a moment, she leaned closer. She pressed her full lips gently against mine for a brief moment, then pulled back just a few millimeters. She was too close for me to see, but I thought I felt her smile. Then she laughed.

"Silly man," she whispered against my lips. "It's going to take a lot more than a stale cup of coffee to get inside these pants."

Disentangling herself from my arms, she stepped back and opened her car door. Then she dropped gracefully into the seat, leaving me standing in the middle of the parking lot with hard-on, looking stupid.

Glancing down, she grinned.

"Impressive," she quipped, then met my eyes once more. "Another time, another place." She slammed the door closed.

"You know you are wrong, right?" Despite my discomfort, I chuckled. "So wrong."

She leaned out the window. "Call your brother, Khalil. He needs you just as much as you need him. You owe this to yourself."

"How did you know?"

"A woman never reveals her sources," she laughed. "But since you were nice enough to buy me a cup of coffee, I'll tell you. Your boy Sanchez told my girl everything." She rolled her eyes. "The things people reveal when they get a little booty."

I took a deep breath and let it out slowly. I couldn't help but feel she was right. I didn't consider myself one to trust people without a long-term trial run first, but something told me I could trust Nicole.

"I'll call him."

"Very good." She started the car. "And don't lose my number again, bad boy."

"I got you."

Still leaning out the window, she beckoned me closer. She reached up as I leaned down, and, grabbing my shirt, she pulled me close, this time kissing me hard and passionately. Letting go, she leaned back and laughed. Then she threw the car in gear, and, before I could even react, she was gone.

# CHAPTER **35**

**Seventy-two hours later,** I still had not mustered the courage to call Todd. Instead of calling, I kept bringing up his number and staring at his name in my contacts list.

"Just call him already." Nicole stared at me from across the room. It had been easy to call her; I'd done it as soon as I got home from Dunkin' Donuts. We had been inseparable since.

Sighing, I kicked my feet up on the coffee table in front of me. My last conversation with Todd hadn't gone well, and I wasn't sure how to turn it around. I still cringed every time I thought about how I'd told him he would be eulogized.

"Look, Khalil." Nicole plopped down on the couch beside me. "I thought you said you wanted to know the truth about where you came from. Well, here's your chance. The truth has found you. His name is Todd Banks. Call him already. I'm sure he's seeking the same answers you are."

Consternation knotted my brow. I did want the truth. But somehow, it didn't seem quite so simple. Interrupting my musing, Nicole climbed on my lap and took my hand into hers. Kissing me lightly on my forehead, she smiled.

"Everything will be fine. I love you, Khalil."

*What!?* That had come out of left field. My mind reeled. I'd barely gotten to know this woman. Admittedly, I'd genuinely enjoyed the past few days. But how was I supposed to respond to "I love you" so soon? As if I weren't already dealing with enough. I glanced quickly at her face, then away, keeping my mouth shut.

Nicole was unfazed by my silence. Instead, still straddling me, she shifted her hips seductively. Immediately, my body began to react.

"You are a bad girl," I whispered.

"Only for you," she promised. She kissed me on the corner of the mouth. "I'm happy we found each other, baby," she sighed, leaning forward and wrapping her arms around my neck. "As they say, all good things come to those who wait." She pulled back again, staring into my eyes with great seriousness. "Khalil, you are my heart's desire and an answered prayer."

This was starting to get seriously weird. "Okay, what is going on?" I asked with skepticism. "Is this confessional time?" I glanced away again but added a small smile, trying to lighten the mood.

"Listen, Khalil." She grabbed my chin and pivoted it towards her. "I'm not here to hurt you. I'm not here to take from you. I'm not here to complicate your life. I'm just trying to tell you I'm here to love and protect that beautiful heart of yours. I'm a true ride-or-die kind of woman. And I got you." She pinned me with an intense stare.

I met her eyes for a moment, then looked away once more, struggling to handle the intensity of the moment and her words. No one had ever said things like that to me before. I had to admit I was touched by her impromptu speech. Despite my misgivings about having only known her a short time, I already trusted her. And I desperately wanted to believe what she was saying.

As I processed my emotions, Nicole continued to watch my face. Finally, I lifted my gaze to meet hers again. I saw nothing but love and trust in her eyes. I took a deep breath, closed my eyes, and slowly exhaled. As I did, I felt something begin to shift deep inside. Slowly, as if a giant fortress were collapsing brick by brick, the walls surrounding my heart began to crumble and fall.

It was terrifying.

Opening my eyes, I looked back at Nicole. She still had me pinned with her intense, serious stare.

"I love you, too." My words echoed in the silent room. *Did I just say that?*

She grinned, kissed me again, then climbed off my lap. Grabbing her purse, she sashayed out of the living room. "Don't go anywhere. I'll be right back," she called over her shoulder.

Seconds later, Nicole returned. She was holding a portable Bose speaker. "I have a surprise for you," she announced.

"I don't know if I've shared this yet, but I don't like surprises."

"Well," she slipped her hand into mine and pulled me to my feet, "I'm pretty sure you will love this one."

"Really?"

"Remember how you saved me from those crazy guys at the club the night we met?"

"Of course. How could I forget?"

"The next day, I waited to hear from you. When you didn't call, I was hurt." Her brow wrinkled briefly, and I frowned. "Still, God told me we would meet again." Her eyes softened as she looked up at me. "So, instead of missing you, I decided to make a playlist of every song that reminded me of you. I've added to it since that day. Can I play it for you?" she asked shyly.

Before meeting Nicole, hearing a woman share something like that would have had me running for the hills. But amazingly, I found I actually wanted to hear what she had compiled.

"Of course," I said. "I would love to."

She smiled. "I love you, Khalil. This is my gift to you." She pushed a few buttons on her phone, then set down the phone and speaker on the coffee table. Without another word, she pulled me closer. As we stood in the middle of the living room holding one another, Destiny's Child's "Cater to You" began to flow through the air.

We swayed gently for a few moments. Then the mood shifted. Nicole pulled me closer, into a tight embrace. I kissed her with fervor, tightening my grip on her waist and pulling her hips close to mine, feeling the heat rising. Breaking the kiss, I noticed her breath was faster and shallow. Time to take things up a notch. With a mischievous grin, I leaned down slightly and swept her off her feet, catching her behind the knees. With sure steps, I headed straight for the bedroom. Laying Nicole across the bed, I kissed her again, feeling her responsiveness.

She looked up at me with dilated eyes. "Make love to me, Khalil," she said, her voice breathy. Sitting up, she reached for the bottom edge of my shirt, pulling it upwards towards my face. I helped pull the shirt over my head, then tossed it to the floor. It was going to be a night of sweet love-making.

I leaned in again, kissing her firmly, enjoying the sensation of her finely manicured nails against my chest. She reached up and wrapped her long, shapely legs around my hips, pulling me down against her. Damn.

"Please, I want you. Take me," she moaned.

"You're sure you want to do this?" I confirmed, already reaching towards my nightstand drawer for protection.

Pulling me forcefully back down, her mouth met mine again. Her lips were amazingly intoxicating.

"I want to. Believe me, I do," she assured me. "But first..." She placed both palms on my chest and pushed me away gently. "...You really should call your brother."

I froze. *Was she kidding?* Surely this wasn't the moment for that. But it was Dunkin' Donuts all over again. *I should've seen it coming,* I chastised myself bitterly. Quickly backing off, I grabbed my shirt from the floor and pulled it roughly back over my head.

"You're not mad, are you?" she asked as I shoved my arms through the sleeves.

"Not at all." I managed to keep my tone neutral, plastering on a fake smile. But I was seriously pissed. *Looks like I'm not getting any until I actually talk to my stupid twin*, I fumed as I retreated to the living room. I knew it wasn't really Todd's fault, but I couldn't help but think I'd be doing something a lot more fun right now if it weren't for him.

SECRET DOOR

# CHAPTER 36

**Nicole trailed behind me** down the hallway then veered off into the kitchen.

"Good luck," she called out. I heard the refrigerator door open.

Before I could even pick up my phone again, she sauntered back into the living room with a bottle of chardonnay and two wine glasses in hand.

"I'm proud of you for doing this. This is a celebratory moment," she smiled, holding up the bottle.

I wasn't sure I agreed. But I nodded anyway, plopping

down on the couch. Unlocking the screen, I tapped my contacts to retrieve Todd's number. Before dialing, I paused. I stared at the digits, trying to collect my thoughts. Noticing my frown, Nicole joined me on the couch.

"Here. Drink this to take the edge off." She popped the cork and poured, then handed me a full glass of wine.

"Thanks," I said, taking a sip. *Not bad,* I thought, allowing the dry wine to trickle down my throat. For a brief moment, the slight burning sensation distracted me from my impending phone call. But taking the edge off would require something a lot stronger than wine. Instead of savoring, I gulped down the rest of the contents.

"Slow down before you get drunk," Nicole laughed, refilling my glass.

"I'm a big boy," I retorted. I took another hearty swig, then put the glass down on the coffee table. Drinking wasn't going to make this any easier. I hadn't even placed the call yet, and I was already feeling emotionally drained. Placing my elbow on my knee, I rested my forehead against the palm of my hand and sighed.

"Look," Nicole said, slipping her arm through mine,

"I'm not going to pretend I know what you are going through. But I can tell you that whenever I'm faced with difficulty, I give it to God. He always makes things right. So... Maybe we should pray."

"Pray?" I lifted my head to look at her, my eyebrows raised. "Ha. The last time I heard a prayer was from the director of the group home when I was sentenced to five years in juvie. Prayer sure didn't help me then. I don't see how praying now is any different." I looked down at my phone, then away, sighing again.

"Well, prayer requires faith. And without faith, Khalil," she paused, her face earnest but serious, "it is impossible to please God."

Hot rage coursed through me instantly. *Please God? Not likely.* I'd sinned way too many times. Besides, what would be the point? God didn't care about me. He'd made that plenty clear.

"Is that so?" I shot back. "Well, it's because of God that I'm stuck here in this predicament," I informed her harshly. "If God had not abandoned me, just like my family and everyone else, maybe praying would help. But not once in my whole life has He shown up for me. So why pray now? He's obviously not going to listen anyway."

Once the words were out of my mouth, I braced for her counter-attack. I'd thrown out some big accusations. But as the seconds dragged on, Nicole still sat there quietly. Slowly, my thoughts started to calm. Unlike so many other people in my life, she wasn't trying to fix me or berate me for my outburst. She was just letting me vent, holding space for my pain and anger.

It was the first time I could remember feeling so supported, seen, and heard. For the first time ever, I felt completely accepted, wounds and all. It was okay to be me, exactly as I was.

With this realization, my anger evaporated.

"Don't get me wrong," I added, my tone calmer now that I knew I didn't have to play defense. I lifted the glass of chardonnay from the table once more and drained it. "I do believe in God. It's just that my faith in Him is... no longer activated. I've been through too much. Praying isn't enough. It's going to take a miracle for me to trust Him again."

"I believe in miracles, Khalil. One day, you will, too."
She shot me a half smile. "I also understand your anger and
frustration," she continued. "It's easy to blame God when
you don't truly understand the plans He has for you. But
God does have plans for you. Plans to prosper and not
harm you, Khalil." She looked at me earnestly.

I stared at her for a moment, wanting to believe her.
But I just couldn't buy it. "If that's the case, then tell me
why I've experienced nothing but harm all my life."

"I can't answer your questions, Khalil. But I know
God can. So, ask Him. Knock and the door will be opened.
Seek and you will find. That's how it goes. Just ask Him."

I frowned. It seemed too simple. Trying to give myself
time to think, I chugged my glass again. Standing up, I took
a deep breath and began pacing the room. If all it took was
asking, I was about to ask a lot.

"Well, then, here's what I want to ask. If His plans
were not to harm me, why didn't He stop my birth
parents from giving me up for adoption? Why let me go to
another dysfunctional family that also didn't want me?
Why not stop my classmates from ridiculing me for being

poor and dark-skinned? I was only ten years old!" I was really working myself up. "Why send me to a group home and then sentence me to juvie for five years? Is this the kind of 'plan' you think God has for me?" By now I was practically shouting.

Still sitting quietly, Nicole took a deep breath in, then she exhaled slowly. Without thinking, I mirrored her actions. Unexpectedly, I felt myself calm back down a bit.

Seeing I'd regained some control, Nicole answered my final question.

"Yes," she said bluntly. "That's exactly what I'm saying. Of course, what happened to you was terrible. Also, it wasn't your fault. But it happened. And without those experiences, you wouldn't be here, in this moment, as the person you are today."

"Okay..." There was some logic there. "But what does that have to do with God?" I wasn't sure I was following.

"Becoming who you are today has prepared you for this moment and so much more. If you are open to it, this can be the moment that God calls you to fulfill the purpose He has for your life."

That seemed like a big claim. I shot her a skeptical

look. "So why is He telling you all this and not me?"

"Because you are not listening to Him. He had to send someone to get your attention, and that someone is me," she stated boldly, her expression intense.

"Whoa," I laughed, pulling back a little. "That was deep."

"This is no joke, KG."

"Oh, so now I'm KG, huh?" I joked again, still trying to lighten the mood.

"No." She rose from the couch to stand in front of me. "KG is what your friends call you, right? Well, since you won't listen to me as your woman, maybe you will listen to me as your friend."

"I'm listening." *Or at least looking*. She sure was fine in those fitted jeans and crop top.

"Tupac has a song called 'Me Against the World.'"

"I love Tupac."

"Stay focused, Khalil. This is not a game."

"But I do love Tupac." This got a laugh out of her.

"So do I, but please let me finish. This is important."

"Okay." I tried to focus.

"It's time for you to let go of everything that has

hindered your growth over the years. It's time to forgive those you believe have hurt you. But even more than that, it's time to forgive yourself."

"Forgive myself?" I repeated, eyebrows raised. What did I need to forgive myself for?

"Yes. You have carried around unforgiveness, anger, and guilt for as long as I have known you... which, admittedly, is not that long. But I know you are not a victim. You are an overcomer. How many people do you know who could have survived your life, including all those challenges and injustices you've been dealt?

"So, when I tell you God has plans for your life, and that everything you've been through is part of it, it's because it's true, and He does. Now get out of your own way already, and let God use your stubborn ass to do some good in the world." Ending her speech, she spun around and dropped back down onto the couch, tucking her legs under her and looking up at me.

For a moment, I was taken aback. Who was she to tell me I wasn't doing my part to make the world a better place? What did she know? I crossed my arms over my chest. *If she wasn't so damn fine,* I thought, *she'd be gone, sent back to wherever she came from.* Then I sighed. I'd already heard her out this far. But did she really think I hadn't done my part? I wasn't the passive type, so I cut to the chase.

"Come on. I've paid my dues to society. Are you really telling me I'm not pulling my weight?"

At this, her face split into a wide grin. "Is that a male ego I'm hearing?" she laughed. "Khalil, all I'm saying is stop blaming the world for your problems. You can either be the problem or you can find the solution. So, man up!"

"Oh, it's like that, huh?"

"Yeah, it is," she said forcefully. "And you're not the only one," she added, obviously irked. "I'm sick and tired of people making excuses for why their lives are messed up. If you don't like the way your life is," she paused briefly, pinning me with another intense stare, "then change it."

I frowned. "Sounds like you've got it all figured out."

"I'm not perfect, Khalil." She rose again and began pacing back and forth in front of me. "We are more alike than you know."

"Really?"

"I may not know what you're going through." She raised her head to look at me, and there were tears in her eyes. "But I understand your pain." As I watched, a tear overflowed and spilled down her cheek. She wiped it away with the back of her hand.

Her show of emotion almost had me convinced. I wanted to believe her, but part of me was still dubious. "Really? Tell me more."

"I grew up in an upper-class neighborhood in Newton. My parents are successful doctors at University Hospital. I have an ivy league education, and to the naked eye, I have it all together, right? But the truth of the matter is, we are one and the same, Khalil."

"One and the same?" I laughed out loud. "We are nothing alike. Our upbringings couldn't have been more different. From where I'm standing, you've lived an all-American life."

"I know how it looks. But despite it all, the truth is, I was incredibly unhappy. I blamed everything and everyone for my own hardships, refusing to believe that changing my own life required a good, hard look in the mirror."

Stepping closer to me, Nicole took my hand in hers. "Don't you think you deserve to be happy?" she asked. I nodded mutely. "I want that for you. God does, too. I also know God has a plan to help you get there. No matter what you've told yourself, He has never abandoned you, Khalil. He has always been there. He is there for you right now. You know what you need. Now, bow your head, and pray."

I watched as she tucked her chin and gently lowered her lashes. She looked so serene. I wanted that kind of peace, too. Maybe she was right. Maybe I *did* need God. At least I could try.

Taking a deep breath, I grasped her hands in return, closed my eyes, and gave it a shot.

"God," I began haltingly, "I'm not going to take up much of Your time or try to hide anything from You, since You're supposed to know everything. But for all these years, I thought You abandoned me, just like everyone else in my life. I have so many questions, all without answers. Why didn't You stop my parents from giving me away?

Why didn't You step in? For most of my life I have been emotionally homeless. The truth is, I didn't think You cared. I didn't think You loved me."

I'd never admitted my fear out loud like that. But saying it somehow made it real. Unexpectedly, a wave of emotion swept over me. My throat tightened, and I found myself fighting back tears. Trying not to let on, I swallowed hard and forged ahead.

"Three days ago, a man claiming to be my brother appeared in my life. I don't know what it all means, but something tells me You do. And I'm ready to find out what that is." Despite my efforts to hold back my emotions, I felt a single tear escape from the corner of my eye and trickle down my cheek. Glancing down, I watched it fall onto Nicole's hand. Oh no, I thought, panicking. My older brothers had taught me a man should never show his emotions in front of a woman. It would make him look soft. But before I could do anything, Nicole opened her eyes and smiled.

"That was beautiful," she told me, her eyes brimming again. Unable to handle the emotional intensity, I pulled away and strode quickly to the kitchen. Resting my palms on the counter, I took several deep breaths. *What just happened out there?* I was feeling things I hadn't felt in years. Trying to get a hold of myself, I took one more deep breath and let it out slowly. It helped a little. I headed back into the living room.

Joining Nicole on the couch, I forced myself to meet her eyes. She was quiet for a moment as she looked at me. Quietly, she said, "I see you, Khalil, and I will never hurt you.".

I felt my body stiffen and reminded myself to breathe. I wanted to believe her. But I'd been promised safety and security before, and every time, I'd ended up with more pain. *Don't buy it. She's just like the rest of them,* I told myself sternly. Despite my self-talk, though, I knew that wasn't the case. Nicole was different. Instead of rejecting her words, I found myself nodding.

Clasping my hands in hers, she added, "I see you, but not everyone can. Maybe you should give your family a break."

*Wait. What?* That was unexpected. "What do you

mean, give them a break?"

"All I mean is that everyone doesn't have the capacity to love us the way we desire. Maybe they gave you all they had to give."

Anger filled me again. My family didn't love me. How could she make claims like that? *I'm the victim, not them.*

Reading my facial expression, she tried to explain. "I'm not trying to downplay what you've been through, Khalil. I just mean the past, which you've been holding onto, left you a long time ago. Maybe it's time you let it go, too." She squeezed my hands, then stared at me for a long moment. Releasing my fingers, she grabbed her purse and keys from the coffee table. "I'll talk to you tomorrow."

Before I could even say goodbye, she was out the door, and I found myself alone with plenty to think about.

# CHAPTER 37

**I wasn't sure I** was ready to face everything Nicole had said. But I knew there was one thing I could do. I grabbed my phone from the coffee table in front of me. It was time to make peace with Todd.

I dialed the number Sanchez had given me, then waited for him to answer.

"Banks residence. Who's calling?"

"Who's this?" I questioned. It was a male voice, but I remembered Todd having a deeper voice like mine. The person on the other line sounded like Mike Tyson. "Let me speak to my brother."

"I think you dialed the wrong number," he responded, slurring. "There is no one by the name of 'let me speak to my brother' that lives here. And what kind of greeting is that, anyway?"

"You did say this was the Banks' residence, right?"

"I did. But like I told you earlier, there is no one by the name of 'let me speak to my brother' that lives here."

I rolled my eyes. Whoever this was, he was clearly intoxicated.

"Put my brother on the phone. Now." I threatened.

"Not until you tell me who you are," he slurred. "Is this Henry, and are you calling for money again?"

"For the last time," I shouted angrily, "put my brother on the phone."

I heard the phone drop, followed by the sounds of someone fumbling around to retrieve it. I sighed impatiently. Finally, the voice returned.

"Oh, I got it. Is this Nephew Tommy from the Steve Harvey Morning Show? It is, isn't it? This is a prank call. Tommy, I should have known it was you."

"This is not the Steve Harvey Morning Show, you

idiot," I yelled. I almost smiled, though. I had to admit, that was funny. "Just tell Todd it's his twin brother, Khalil."

"What do you mean you're his twin brother?" Just then, I heard another voice in the room. It sounded like Todd.

"Who is Khalil?" the drunken voice asked. "And why is he saying he's your twin brother?"

"I'll explain it to you later." Todd cleared his throat. "What's up, Khalil? What do you want?"

"We need to talk. Are you available tonight?"

"Meet me at the Violet Lounge in an hour," Todd said. "See you there."

# CHAPTER 38

**As I zipped in** and out of traffic on I-93, a red pick-up truck careened down the speed lane, narrowly missing my bike. I honked my irritation and violently sped after him. I flashed my lights repeatedly, tailing hard, when I heard a voice say, "Let it go."

Unsure whether the voice came from God or if I was just hearing things, I quickly complied and pulled off at the next exit, back en route to the Violet Lounge. *Hm. That was new.* By the time I reached the Violet Lounge, though, the incident was forgotten.

The night was hot, but it hadn't stopped the crowd from showing up. As I drove up, I searched the long entry line for Todd. There was no way I was going to wait for that. Instead, I pulled up for VIP service. The valet greeted me. "May I help you?"

"Can I get VIP service for my motorcycle?" I asked as I reached for the clasp to unhook my helmet. I knew it was a long shot as the sign on the side of the Violet Lounge read, "Cars Only."

Before he could answer, a short, white guy with a receding hairline stomped up to us, frowning at my bike.

"He's looking for VIP service for his motorcycle," the valet explained unnecessarily.

"The sign clearly says 'cars only.' Tell him that VIP service is only for vehicles and not motorcycles," he instructed loudly. Never meeting my eyes, he turned back towards the club. "Some people," he muttered, shaking his head as he walked away.

*As expected. But where there's a will, there's a way.* Pulling my helmet off, I called after him. "Excuse me, sir?" I removed a crisp hundred from my wallet and extended it.

His eyes grew wide when he saw it, and he finally looked up and met my gaze. Seeing my face, his jaw dropped. Scurrying towards me, he quickly took the money and began apologizing profusely. "I'm so sorry," he rushed out. "I didn't know it was you." Retrieving a black-and-gold card with the letters "VIP" printed on it, he handed it to me as he continued his apology. "Please forgive me, sir. You can park right across the street in the spot labeled VIP."

If this was the kind of treatment Todd was used to receiving, I didn't mind playing along. I slipped the VIP card into my wallet and pulled into the parking lot with a grin on my face. This night was really coming together.

With my helmet in tow, I darted across the street towards the Violet Lounge. An attractive white woman wearing a sexy green dress that hugged her body like a glove scurried up to me.

"Hey, baby!" She wrapped her arms around my neck and inhaled. "Is this a new cologne you're wearing?" she asked, pressing her breast against my shoulder. "And that helmet? I didn't know you rode a motorcycle."

With her body up against mine, I'd forgotten for a

second that I had an identical twin. I laughed to myself as her comments finally registered. *Must be one of Todd's lady friends*, I thought, disentangling myself and heading for the front of the line. Green Dress trailed behind me.

"I know I can come off a little aggressive sometimes." She took a couple of quick steps to come up alongside me, wrapping her arm tightly around mine and holding on tight with her other hand. Digging in her heels, she pulled me to a stop, then leaned in to press her lips against the side of my neck. "You do know you can have me whenever you want, right?" she whispered.

As attractive an offer as that was, I needed to draw the line before she started taking her clothes off. "Listen," I grabbed her shoulders and held her back. "You obviously have me confused with somebody else. Why don't you be a good girl and keep it moving."

"What's wrong with you?" she hissed. "I don't know why you're acting brand new. Just because you go to church doesn't mean you can talk to me like that."

"No disrespect, snow bunny." I handed the VIP card and my driver's license to the three-hundred-pound bouncer standing in front of the velvet rope. "You're fine and all that, but I'm not into white girls."

"You weren't talking the other day when we were kissing in the restaurant parking lot." Without waiting for my response, she turned and began to saunter her way to the back of the line. After a few steps, she stopped, turned, and smiled at me seductively. "My offer still stands, Mr. Jungle Fever."

I rolled my eyes, stepping past the velvet rope the bouncer held out for me. Inside, I circled the club for Todd but didn't see him. I nestled up at the bar and checked the time. It was 11:30 PM. I was a little early.

Fifteen minutes later, I felt a hand hit my shoulder. Turning around, I saw Todd. He wasn't alone.

"Khalil?" he greeted me. "This is my boy, *Blake Harden*."

Time screeched to a halt as I stared into the face of the punk who'd landed me in juvie nearly fifteen years ago. His pompous ass stood mere inches from me, smiling. My jaw clamped together hard as I reigned in my anger. I felt like a ticking bomb about to explode.

"It's the Doublemint twins," he shouted. "So, you are

261

Todd's long-lost brother, huh? If I didn't see the two of you standing here, I would never have believed Todd had an ugly-ass twin." He laughed loudly.

I gritted angrily at him but didn't utter a word.

"Bartender," he called. "Can I get six Bacardi shots and three Heinekens?" He dropped a fifty spot on the bar. Tossing back two of the shots, he looked at me. "What's your last name again?"

"Gilliam. It's Khalil Gilliam." I grabbed one of the shots and tipped it back, contemplating my revenge.

"Why does your name sound so familiar?" He reached for a Heineken.

Not waiting for my response, he slammed his fist down on the bar and called the bartender back over. "Two more shots," he ordered. "I'm gonna let the two of you get caught up. Besides, there are too many fine ladies in here for me to be hanging out with the twin towers." He threw back the two shots the bartender placed before him, one after the other, then lifted the Heineken from the bar and chugged it. Seconds later, he descended onto the dance floor.

With Blake gone, Todd downed his shots. "So, what do you wanna talk about?"

The music inside the club was too loud. "Let's take a walk outside to talk."

Grabbing my helmet and jacket from the bar stool, we headed toward the exit of the Violet Lounge. I could feel the stares on us as we walked through the crowd.

Crossing over to the VIP parking lot, I laid my helmet and jacket on the seat of my motorcycle. "I wanna apologize for the way I acted the other day. Up until a few weeks ago, I didn't even know you existed. This is a lot for me to take in, but, if you're open to it, I want to get to know you. I'm willing to give it a try."

"That's all I want, too," he smiled. "Oh, and that guy you nearly killed inside the warehouse?"

"Yeah, I thought that crackhead was trying to set me up. It served him right."

"Well, that so-called crackhead is your older brother Henry."

"What?" I was shocked. "Henry is our brother?"

"Yes. That's what I was trying to tell you that day."

"Damn," I shook my head. "When will all of these secrets end?"

"If it wasn't for Henry, you and I would have never met. He is the one who told me about you. And don't worry. You didn't kill him. He will recover."

"Thank God." I smiled.

"Now that we are on speaking terms," he circled my bike, admiring it, "are you ready to meet the rest of the family?"

"One step at a time." I was still trying to put all the pieces together.

"Sure. When you are ready," he nodded his agreement. "It's nice to finally meet you, brah." He leaned in for a quick hug.

"You too."

Knowing we'd talk again soon, I slipped on my motorcycle jacket and helmet and straddled the bike, revving the engine as Todd stepped back. "One last thing," I called out as I backed out of the parking spot.

"What's that?"

"Your friend, Blake?"

"What about him?"

"He's bad news. Don't trust him. He is a snake." Twisting the throttle, I peeled out of the parking lot.

# CHAPTER 39

**Over the next few weeks,** Todd and I got to know each other better, connecting by phone, text messages, and even face-to-face. But I was still leery of the khaki-wearing attorney. Even though we were cut from the same cloth, I didn't trust him. What made him any different from my birth family? Or even my adoptive family? If none of them wanted a relationship with me, why should he?

Nicole and I were watching Netflix at her home in the uppity town of Newton when my phone rang.

"Hello?"

"What's up, brah? It's Todd."

"Watching a movie with my girl." I stepped out onto the patio. "What's up?"

"The Boston Celtics are playing the Toronto Raptors tonight and I got floor seats," his voice rang with excitement. "Meet me at TD Garden in an hour."

Nicole joined me on the patio. "Is everything okay?" she mouthed in a hushed tone.

I nodded yes and hit the mute button on my iPhone. "Todd just invited me to the Celtics game tonight."

"I hope you said yes!" She wrapped her arms around my neck and kissed me hard.

"What was that for?"

"I'm so proud of you, Khalil." Kissing me a second time, she traced the side of my face gently with her fingertips, then headed back into the living room. I watched her go, appreciating the sway of her hips as she sauntered away.

"You still there?"

I unmuted the phone. "Yeah. I'm here. And I'm down."

"Excellent. See you in an hour, Khalil."

Todd was standing in the lobby of the Garden with a group of well-dressed white men when I arrived. Wearing his signature khakis with a green blazer with a black-and-green Boston Celtics t-shirt underneath, he was dressed much as I expected - except for the pair of construction Timberland boots on his feet. It was a nice but unorthodox touch for a high-priced attorney. It surprised me to discover I was proud he and I were wearing the same footwear.

"I'm glad you agreed to join me." He hugged me in greeting. It was a gesture I wasn't comfortable with, but I hugged him back. He was my brother, after all.

After introducing me to the well-dressed gentlemen who turned out to be his colleagues, we headed to our seats.

"I hope you're ready to be entertained." Todd handed our tickets to the arena staff. "It's going to be a great game."

Walking through the metal detectors resurrected painful memories of the detention center. I held my poker face but cringed on the inside at the memories. Nicole had told me to let go of the past, but those old internal scars remained. I couldn't seem to escape them.

"Everything okay?" Todd asked, noticing my uneasiness.

"Yeah, I'm good," I lied. I hadn't shared my past with Todd. Now certainly wasn't the right time or place, and despite our matching faces, he was still a stranger.

A gorgeous brown-skinned woman with long dreadlocks led us to our seats, but before we could get settled, Todd got a phone call. "Sorry," he mouthed as he stepped away.

It was my first visit to the Garden, and I was impressed by the numerous championship banners and retired players' names and numbers hanging from the rafters. We were as close to the court as you could get, but there really wasn't a bad seat in the house. The security around the court was no joke, though. There were enough armed guards present to protect the White House.

Suddenly, a thunderous roar erupted from the Garden's crowd as Kyrie Irving and Jalen Brown stepped onto the court for pregame warmups. As Irving put on a dribbling exhibition for the fans, an attractive brunette white woman wearing a short-sleeved, black-and-green shirt and black pants approached me.

"Hi, Mr. Banks," she smiled. "I like your beard. It looks great on you."

*Another one who thinks I'm Todd.* Instead of bursting her bubble and telling her I was Todd's twin, I played along.

"Thanks," I said with a devilish grin. "I've been growing it for some time now."

Dropping her hand on my shoulder, she squeezed. "Somebody has been working out."

I laughed to myself as I scanned the menu. *These white girls are crazy.*

"Don't tell me," she leaned in. "A Heineken with a classic burger and steak fries?"

Just as I was about to agree, Todd returned.

"Hey there," he greeted her. "I see you've met my twin brother, Khalil."

"Twin?" she peered over at me and then back at Todd. "I didn't know you had a twin, Mr. Banks."

"Neither did I," he laughed.

"Your brother had me going!" She playfully jabbed me on the side of the arm. "Please tell me you're single."

Opening my phone, I flashed a picture of Nicole.

Still smiling, she lowered her head to my ear. "She is gorgeous, but that still doesn't answer my question."

"I'm sure a woman as attractive as you doesn't have a problem meeting good guys."

"I'm not looking for a good guy," she flirted, still leaning in. "I'm looking for the perfect connection with a bad boy like you." Squeezing my shoulder again, she winked and walked away.

"But what about our food and drinks?" I called out.

"We're all set," Todd laughed. "She's feeling you, brah."

Moments later, she returned carrying a large tray.

"Two classic burgers, steak fries and Heinekens for the twins. That will be $57.44."

"I got this." Todd reached inside his wallet and removed an invitation-only black American Express card.

After he signed the receipt, she thanked him for the generous tip. Before exiting, she turned towards me and slipped a folded napkin into my hand. "Use this if you ever decide you want to venture over to the wild side."

I tossed the napkin under my seat.

Glancing at his phone, Todd frowned, then stood. "I'll be right back." He headed towards the exit. Shrugging, I dug into my food.

The Garden was at full capacity when Todd returned a few minutes later. He was not alone.

*What is he doing here?*

"You remember Blake, from the club a few weeks ago?"

"How could I forget?" I could hear my bitter tone, but I couldn't help it. I was seeing red. I downed the rest of my Heineken and flagged down arena staff for something stronger.

"Kareem, right?" Blake joked. "The second half of the infamous Siamese twins?"

I wished we were somewhere less crowded so I could deliver the punch to Blake's face that he sorely deserved. But the Garden sat over nineteen thousand, and it looked like a completely full house. *Way too many witnesses.* Instead, I locked down my anger, stood, and casually took a few steps towards him. Just then, Todd's phone rang again. "Sorry, gotta take this." Putting the phone to his ear, he stepped away from us, turned his back, and began talking animatedly.

Plastering on a smile, I extended my hand to shake Blake's. Keeping my tone low so Todd wouldn't hear, I grabbed his hand hard and said harshly, "I guess that ass-whipping I gave you all those years ago didn't teach you anything, huh?"

Blake's jaw dropped. "No way," he whispered, staring at me. Wrenching his hand out of mine, he glanced around the arena, then back at me, clearly acknowledging all our witnesses. Reaching for his drink, he said casually, "Shouldn't you be in Rikers Island, you criminal?" With a grin, he plopped back down in his seat.

Who did he think he was talking to? Leaning in, I put my hand on the armrest next to his seat. In a low, angry voice I hoped wouldn't carry, I threatened, "When the time is right, *Blake Harden*, I'm going to beat you until you can't remember your own name."

"Threatening me in front of all these witnesses doesn't seem wise," he shook his head. "I'm sorry to see that after all these years, you are still the same punk you were in the group home. They should have buried your ass under the jail. Now sit your ex-con butt down before I tell Todd the truth about you."

Returning from his phone call, Todd approached us

with a frown on his face. "Everything okay?"

"For now," I gritted at Blake.

The buzzer for the game sounded exactly at 7:30 PM. The announcer introduced both teams. After the national anthem, the starters from each team walked to center court for the official tip-off.

Blake was mean-mugging me when I decided to text Sanchez to give him the 411.

*I'm at the Celtics game with my brother Todd. Can you believe he invited Blake?*

*Did you know he was coming?*

*Hell no. If I did, I would have declined.*

*If you need me, just say the word, and I'm there.*

*Much respect, but I got this.*

*Try to enjoy the game and don't let that punk get under your skin.*

*Respect. Can you believe he called me Kareem?*

*LOL! That's kind of funny, KG.*

*Peace, Sanchez.*

*Peace, Kareem!*

At half-time, Blake got up and stretched. "Okay, Mary-Kate and Ashley," he laughed. "I'll be right back. Got to drain the main vein."

Already boiling, his Mary-Kate comment pushed me over the edge. Everything I felt over the years was staring me in the face. This was the day Blake Harden was going to pay for his past indiscretions.

The burn inside intensified as I watched him exit the arena. "I'll be right back," I tossed out to Todd. I hurried out of the arena after Blake without waiting for his response.

I watched from a distance as Blake made small talk with one of the guys Todd had introduced me to earlier. After their brief encounter, he pushed the bathroom door open. I quickly followed. I was aiming for the element of surprise, but he spotted me in the mirrors. I had to act fast. Forcing him inside one of the stalls, I locked my right arm around his neck and squeezed.

"I told you your day was coming."

Looking towards the open stall door, Blake fought to free himself. His resistance only increased my anger. As I tightened my grip a bit more, he flailed harder, but to no avail. I could see the white of his eyes now. When foam started appearing at the corners of his mouth, I knew he was about to pass out.

"Go to sleep," I whispered. I squeezed even harder until his body went limp.

Just then, the bathroom door flung open. Quickly reaching for the stall door, I grabbed it from underneath and pulled it closed.

"Who's in there?" a patron called out. "Are you okay?"

"Yeah, I'm fine," I shot back. "My friend is piss-drunk. He is puking all over the place."

"Should I call for help?"

"Thanks, buddy," I said in my whitest voice. "But he's fine." In the distance, the buzzer for the second half sounded.

"I hope your friend is okay."

"Thanks, pal." Reaching up, I twisted the lock closed, then lowered Blake on the pissy bathroom floor. Waiting until the other guy left, I dunked Blake's head into the toilet repeatedly. "Drink up," I whispered.

Before I knew what was happening, he snapped

awake. Shoving himself back from the toilet, Blake screamed bloody murder. *Damn!* Somebody surely heard that. I dashed out of the bathroom, rushing towards our seats. I had to get there before Blake did.

I was no more than a hundred feet away when I saw Blake and a police officer closing in quickly. With no time to spare, I rushed towards Todd, grabbed my jacket from the back of my chair, and announced, "I have to go."

"What's wrong?"

Over his shoulder, I could see Blake and the officer closing in. "My boy's car broke down on I-93." I lied.

"But I have to ask you something."

"I'll call you later." I beelined it out of the arena. As I reached the exit, I breathed a sigh of relief. Then I smiled widely. I'd given Blake a tiny taste of what he'd given me, and it felt damn good.

# CHAPTER 40

**My elation at my bit of** revenge lasted about ten minutes into my drive home. I knew Blake wasn't the one whose actions had landed me in the group home. That had been my own doing. Even the fight that had sent me to the detention center hadn't been started by him. I'd done that, too. It was just that the rage overtook me sometimes... When that happened, it felt like the chokehold it had on me was more violent than anything I'd ever unleashed on Blake.

Maybe Nicole was right. Maybe I *did* need God. Hell if I knew. One thing seemed sure, though. If I didn't get a hold of my anger, I would end up back in confinement.

When I finally arrived home, I pulled into my parking spot and sat there, trying to figure out my next move. Before I could even contemplate my options, my cell phone buzzed. It was Todd.

"Hello." It had to be about Blake.

"You hurried out of the stadium so quickly, I didn't get a chance to ask you," he panted.

"Ask me what?" I wondered what had him breathing so hard.

"I'm getting married, and I want you to be one of my groomsmen. Can I count on you to be there for me?"

I was surprised but honored. "Whatever you need, I got you," I said. "But I didn't know you were seeing anyone, let alone engaged."

There was silence for a moment. "It was a secret," he offered with a laugh. "It happened suddenly."

"Suddenly, huh?" Something about that sounded off. I needed to know more. "When do I get to meet this wonderful woman?"

"Tomorrow night at the rehearsal dinner, if you can make it," he said.

"When is the wedding?"

"On Saturday."

"*This* Saturday?"

"Yessir," he laughed. "I just texted you the time and location. Oh, and one last thing. Your tuxedo fitting is scheduled for tomorrow at 1:00 PM. I just sent that text, too."

Seemed like he had it all together. Before I ended the call, I asked one last question. "How was the rest of the game?"

"You missed a hell of a game. The Celtics squeaked out the win."

"Sorry I missed it. But my boy needed me. You know how that goes, right?"

"Is he okay?"

"Yeah, he's good."

"Okay, cool."

"I'll see you tomorrow."

"Wait," he paused. "Blake wants to speak to you."

I heard rustling as the phone was handed over. Then there was silence for a few moments before Blake's voice came on the line. "Your time is coming, Kareem," he said in a hushed tone. "Payback is going to be a mother..."

"Is that a threat?" I interrupted, my anger spiking once more.

"It's a promise."

I couldn't believe this punk. "How did that piss taste?" I asked, laughing out loud. Without waiting for an answer, I hung up. Blake was not done paying for his misdeeds.

# CHAPTER 41

**The following morning,** I met Nicole at the Silver Slipper restaurant for breakfast. Located in the heart of Boston, the Silver Slipper was known for its exquisite Jamaican cuisine. As I entered the well-known establishment, I spotted Nicole at the back of the restaurant, seated near a well-dressed older couple.

Glued to her phone, she didn't look up until I was nearly at the table. Glancing up, her warm brown eyes met mine, and her face lit up with her beautiful smile. She stood up to greet me, and I pulled her close.

"I love you, Mr. Gilliam," she whispered. Then her soft lips collided with mine. I smiled into her kiss. I'd never been one for public affection, but with Nicole, everything seemed right. *Could she be the one?*

Wearing a gorgeous navy blue dress that showed off the shape of her body, I knew every man in the house was looking her way. "You look amazing today," I flirted.

"This old thing?" She gave a dismissive wave. Then she noticed me staring at the price tag still dangling from the side of the dress. She crinkled her nose as she realized she'd been caught, then grinned at me.

"Well, old or new," I smirked, "you look great."

"Before you get all mushy, let's eat." I couldn't say no to that. Simultaneously, we unfolded our menus.

Seconds later, a petite, dark-skinned woman with long box braids greeted us. "Welcome to the Silver Slipper. My name is Monique, and I will be your server today." Sliding her glasses down to the tip of her nose, she locked eyes with me, completely ignoring Nicole. But Nicole noticed her.

"Nice to meet you, Monica," Nicole clawed.

"It's Monique!"

"Excuse me?"

"My name is Monique, not Monica," she said with an attitude.

"Well Monica, I'm Nicole, and that fine piece of chocolate across the table is *my* man, Khalil."

*Her man?* Apparently our relationship had reached the title level. Maybe this was her way of marking her territory to keep the unknowns out. Before things got ugly, I decided to step in.

"Do you have any breakfast specials today?" I asked, pretending to peruse the menu.

"I'm glad you asked," she smirked at Nicole. "Today's breakfast special is porridge, dumplings, callaloo, salt fish, plantains, and we also have fresh carrot juice and mint tea."

Nicole looked at me and laughed. "I'll have a veggie omelet and a cup of ginger tea," she ordered.

"And for the gentleman?"

"I'll have fried dumplings, callaloo, salt fish and plantains."

Nicole shook her head.

"And for your drink?"

"Coffee and water will do."

"Right away." She turned and headed towards the kitchen.

"When was the last time you had a home-cooked meal, Khalil?"

"The last time I visited my mother's house."

"Well, a man like you deserves to be taken care of in every way. My mother always told me the way to a man's heart was through his stomach."

Before I could respond, the waitress was back with our drinks.

"Ginger tea for the lady, and a cup of java for the handsome gentleman. Your meal will be ready shortly. Ciao."

I picked up where we'd left off. "Well, maybe one day I will be lucky enough to find someone as wonderful as you to be my ride or die... in the kitchen and beyond."

"One day?" She raised her eyebrows. "What do you think this is?" she asked, gesturing to the two of us.

Something told me I was about to find out. "We're having breakfast," I joked halfheartedly.

"I love you, Khalil, and I am ready to spend the rest

of my life with you. You are the one for me." Nicole spoke honestly and openly.

I leaned back in my seat, trying to take in the abrupt dive into emotional territory. No one had ever expressed their true feelings for me this way. I still didn't know what to do or how to respond when she was so open and vulnerable, but I knew I didn't want to live without her. Taking a deep breath, I reached for her hand and did my best to follow suit. "Never in a million years did I believe I would find a woman as amazing as you."

I overheard the older woman seated at the table next to us whispering loudly to her husband. "I think he's going to propose!"

The tension in the room was thick. "I love you, Nicole. You are the love of my life. I, too, want to spend my life with you. But can it wait until after Todd's wedding tomorrow?"

"What?" Her eyes widened as she pulled back. "Todd's getting married?"

285

# CHAPTER 42

**It was 7:15 PM** when I pulled into the parking garage of the Ritz Carlton hotel. Running late, I quickly parked my motorcycle in an empty spot next to a white Mercedes Benz with New York plates. Swinging my leg off the bike, I straightened out my clothes. I was digging my all-black ensemble, but I still couldn't believe I had agreed to being one of Todd's groomsmen, especially since I knew my archenemy Blake was also one.

I took a deep breath and stepped inside the luxurious hotel. A quick word with the front desk pointed me in the right direction. As I parted the double doors to the ballroom where the rehearsal dinner was taking place, I spotted Todd sitting at a table with several others in the center of the room. Seeing him, I was glad I'd shown up.

Then I spotted Blake nearby. A sour taste filled my mouth.

Trying to ignore my nemesis, I sauntered towards the table to greet Todd. An attractive, gray-haired woman stopped me. "Pastor Patterson is one lucky woman to have landed such a handsome man," she exclaimed. She wrapped one arm around my neck and, with the other, reached down and squeezed my derrière. "If it doesn't work out with the Pastor, call me."

Before the old cougar could sink in her claws any farther, I freed myself from her grasp and beelined it towards Todd. As I neared him, I glanced over my shoulder and shuddered. *If that was any indication, this is going to be a long night.*

When I finally reached Todd, he greeted me with a brotherly hug.

"I'm glad you could make it," his voice rang with excitement. "You remember Blake, of course." He nodded in Blake's direction.

"Yeah, I remember him," I said, tossing a disdainful look his way.

"So the evil twin decided to crash the party, huh?" Blake laughed. "And what's up with the ninja outfit? You plan on robbing a convenience store when you leave here?"

I clenched my fists by my side and narrowed in on his jaw. "You think you're funny?"

Before I could break his jaw, Todd grabbed me by the back of the arm. "Let me introduce you to my fiancée," he said, guiding me over a few tables to a woman chatting with an elderly man. "Chloe, this is my brother, Khalil."

At the sound of her name, the woman spun in her chair. "Holy mother of God," she breathed. Excitedly, she stood and leaned in for a hug. Pulling back, she held the sides of my arms and looked at me closely. "You were not joking when you said the two of you were identical. It is so good to meet you, Khalil. Where have you been hiding all these years?"

*In the gutter.* The thought arose unbidden. Shoving it away, I smiled. "It's nice to meet you, too." Todd was right. Chloe was a head-turner, easily the most beautiful woman in the room. Her long, black hair flowed over her shoulders, and her smile was perfect. For a brief moment, I completely forgot Nicole. Then, over Chloe's shoulder, I saw Blake mean-mugging me again. Discreetly, I stuck up my middle finger at him. I knew it was a childish act, but I didn't care.

After a few more formal introductions, Todd dragged me away from his soon-to-be family and towards the bar. "Two Heinekens, please."

"So, what do you think of my fiancée?" he smiled. "She's beautiful, isn't she?"

I shrugged. "Looks fade."

He frowned. "What is that supposed to mean?"

I didn't want to be the one to burst his bubble, but since he'd asked, I went on. "It's the good-looking ones that are the most trouble." I took a swig of my beer. "You did say she's a pastor, right?"

"Yeah, she's a pastor." His tone was concerned. "Do you think I'm making a mistake by getting married?"

I looked at him, eyebrows raised. I hadn't said that at all. "It sounds like you have doubts, bruh."

"I don't have doubts," he said hastily, glancing towards Chloe, who was beaming as she conversed with an older couple. "But... It has only been seven months."

I looked him square in the eye. "If you don't want to marry her, then call it off."

"Call it off?" A trace of panic entered his voice. "It's not that easy," he backpedaled.

"Why not?" I chugged the rest of my beer.

"Because everyone here is counting on me. How can I possibly let so many people down?"

"Let them down? These people don't know you. This is your life. Why are you asking for permission to live it? To hell with these fake people." I could tell by the look in his eye that my comment hit home. But I also saw the fear lingering there. I knew the problem. My brother was a people-pleaser.

"What will everyone think if I call off the wedding now?"

Turning on my bar stool to face him, I dropped my hands on his shoulders. "The real question is, how will you live with yourself if you betray who you really are? Isn't that more important than trying to please these phony people?"

"I'm not trying to please anyone!" he exclaimed loudly. "Especially the people in this room," he added more quietly.

"Sure. If that's true, then tell me this. When was the last time you made a decision for yourself?"

He frowned at me. "I have made plenty," he pushed out. But he stumbled over the words.

"Okay then, let's hear one," I challenged. I flagged the bartender for another beer.

The beer arrived, but Todd still had nothing. I swigged several times while he sat there, rubbing his head and staring into space. Finally, I called him out again. "You are a liar, bruh. You have been living for others while lying to and fooling yourself. This may be your rehearsal dinner, but your life is not a dress rehearsal. Take off the mask and start living your life."

He stared at me.

Slipping off the stool, I left Todd at the bar to contemplate my brotherly wisdom and headed for the men's room. By the time I returned to the bar, he was back in the crowd. I ordered another beer, laughing as I watched the black Trumps dancing offbeat to the "Cha-Cha Slide."

I felt my cell phone buzz in my pocket and pulled it out to see a message from Nicole.

*Hey baby. I hope you're having a great time at the rehearsal dinner. I'm still out with the girls, but we're wrapping up soon. I just wanted you to know how much I miss you. I love you. Call me later.*

I felt myself relax as I read. I sent back a quick *Will do*, noticing how Nicole's message had put me at ease. My thoughts of slapping Blake around had somehow disappeared.

"Would you like another?" The bartender grabbed the empty bottle in front of me and slipped it under the bar. I nodded. As he placed a new bottle in front of me, Blake strolled up.

"Listen," I stopped him in his tracks. "It's not the time or the place."

"No disrespect," he sat on the barstool next to me. "We're not kids anymore, Khalil. Let's let bygones be bygones, deal?" He stretched his arm out.

I hadn't expected that. And I wasn't sure I believed him. Would he really let it go, especially after what I'd done to him in the Garden bathroom? Was this just another ploy against me? *Maybe I should punch him in the face for good measure.* But I'd just cautioned him against making a scene, and taking him down now would certainly cause one. And... Maybe he was right. Maybe it was time to bury the hatchet. Either way, my answer was the same. Rolling my eyes, I reluctantly shook his hand.

Downing the last of the Heineken, I turned to face him. Though his physical appearance had changed, his eyes were still the size of golf balls. He turned to face me as well, weaving a bit on his stool.

"Why did you do it?"

"Do what?" he demanded drunkenly. "What are you talking about?"

"You're telling me you don't remember?" I wanted to blame his lack of memory on the alcohol, but this went way farther back. "The day I got kicked out of the group home. It was you and that punk Leon's fault."

"You got it all wrong, Khalil."

"Everyone knows Leon started the fight," I said with an attitude. "And if you would have stayed out of it and not snitched, I would have never gone to juvie."

"What makes you think it was me who snitched?" Waving at the bartender, he ordered four shots. "It wasn't me."

"Of course it was you! If not you, who else?" I shouted in anger.

"After all these years, you still don't know, do you?" He laughed darkly and downed two of the shots back to back. "It was your long-time friend Sanchez. He was behind the whole thing." Picking up the other two shots, Blake headed for the dance floor, leaving me with my jaw hanging open in disbelief.

# CHAPTER 43

**I stood outside the church,** looking up at the large gold cross, willing myself to go in. I'd never thought I'd see the day I'd attend a family wedding, let alone be in one. The only time I had seen the inside of a church was on TV.

To top it off, it was also the first time I was going to see my real family. They'd be able to recognize me because of my brother, but since they hadn't been part of the rehearsal dinner, I still didn't know who they were. I suddenly wished I'd taken Todd up on his offer to meet them sooner. Now it was too late.

I looked at my phone once more, hoping it would ring or show a message from Sanchez letting me know he was back in town. I needed to get to the bottom of what Blake had said. I didn't want to believe Sanchez was a traitor. But so much of my life had been built on lies that I wasn't going to leave another stone unturned. I needed the truth.

I adjusted the lapel of my tux, took a deep breath, and parted the double doors of the church. Stepping inside, I located the staircase and quickly headed up, hoping to find the second-floor room where I was supposed to meet Todd. But I was waylaid as soon as I made it up the stairs.

"Congratulations, Todd," an older white couple greeted me, capturing me from either side in a tight hug. I tried to protest, but they wouldn't hear it. The smell of cheap perfume and cologne was suffocating.

Heading down the hallway, I received at least four more congratulations from strangers who thought I was my brother. A few people even slipped me monetary gifts meant for the happy couple. Tired of protesting, I finally gave up and just let them believe I was Todd. *Should've seen it coming.* My shared face made it impossible for me to be left alone.

I felt another hand drop on my shoulder. This time it was Blake, laughing like a maniac at my repeatedly mistaken identity.

"Todd sent me to find you, but maybe it should be you getting married, not your brother," he joked. "We're due in the sanctuary. This way." I wasn't exactly glad to see him, but I was working on being cool with him, at least until I heard the truth from Sanchez.

We lined up with the other groomsmen, waiting for the ceremony to begin. Blake bragged loudly about which bridesmaid he would sleep with. Tempting as it was to tell him to shut the hell up, I tuned his comments out. Instead, my mind replayed our conversation from the previous night. *How could Sanchez be behind it all?* No matter how many times I reviewed the incidents that had happened all those years ago, I couldn't piece together how it was Sanchez's fault.

I was snapped out of my musing when the sanctuary doors opened. The pastor who would be officiating entered and headed down the aisle. Todd followed closely behind him. He was a sweaty mess.

"What's wrong with Todd?" one of the groomsmen whispered.

As Todd stepped up to take his place, I heard Blake say something about sleeping with Chloe and how Todd was getting his sloppy seconds. I raised my eyebrows. Pivoting to Todd, the worried look on his face confirmed it was true.

"I guess you gave up hope on your dream girl from the train, huh? What was her name again?" Blake continued.

"London," Todd replied in a low voice. My eyebrows shot up even further. The situation was more complicated than I'd thought.

"I told you he was a snake," I nodded in Blake's direction. "Don't worry, bruh. I got you."

Before the bride could enter the church, I stepped off my post and approached Todd. "What are you doing?" he mouthed nervously.

"Listen," My tone was all business. "If you don't want to get married today, then you don't have to. To hell with what all of these phonies in this church think. This is your life, and only you can choose. But if you betray your conscience by marrying a woman you don't love and don't want to marry, just know it will be no one's fault but your own.

"Seriously, bruh. When are you going to stop giving your power to others?" I pressed. "I don't want to see you throw your life away. You've got to stand up on your own two feet and make your own decisions." Chloe was beautiful, but not beautiful enough to marry if she wasn't the one. I'd tried warning him at the rehearsal dinner, but I wasn't sure I'd gotten through. I just hoped he'd step up before it was too late.

"I know," Todd replied. His eyes shifted over my shoulder. I followed his gaze to an older woman in the crowd.

"Who's that?" I asked.

"It's Mom."

*She's beautiful.* An unexpected wave of emotion took over. "And the two ladies next to her?"

"Your sisters," he confirmed.

The pastor cleared his throat angrily. "Can you get back to your post? The bride will be appearing soon."

I glared at him but stepped back in line. "Think about what I said," I urged. From my designated spot, I stared at my mother and sisters. I saw Henry standing at the back of the church next to a giant of a man. "Who is the guy standing next to Henry?" I interrupted Blake, who was still carrying on about banging bridesmaids.

Turning to me, he smiled. "That's your brother, Derek."

After so many years, I never thought I'd be this close to my birth family. But here I was. They were all staring at me, too, smiling. My birth mother's eyes were filled with tears.

"I'm sorry," she mouthed to me. "I love you, Khalil." Tears burned my eyes. It was exactly what I needed to hear. But I refused to let my emotions take over. My anger and resentment had not completely disappeared. I'd still been abandoned at birth.

I sighed and turned back to Todd. His head was bowed, and his fingers were locked together. His lips were moving, but I couldn't hear a sound. Was he praying?

He opened his eyes and looked at me.

Seconds later, the sanctuary doors opened, revealing

Chloe, escorted by the man I assumed was her father. The pianist began the bridal processional, and they stepped forward, beginning the long walk down the aisle. I shifted my focus back to Todd. His doubts had been replaced by a smile brighter than the noonday sun.

"She is so beautiful," he sighed to himself. "And I'm the luckiest man in the world."

"Do not be fooled by her good looks," I reminded him in a loud whisper. "This is your life you're choosing."

"Who gives this woman to be married to this man?" the pastor asked as they arrived in front of the altar.

"I do," Chloe's father said proudly. Removing her hand from his arm, he planted a soft kiss to Chloe's forehead. "I love you, baby girl."

"I love you too, Daddy."

Glancing out over the crowd, I saw Nicole sitting in the back pew. As our eyes met, she shot me an encouraging smile and mouthed, "I love you."

I smiled in return but quickly turned my attention back to Todd. My brother needed me. He was about to make the biggest mistake of his life.

After a prayer and a brief sermon, the pastor closed his Bible. "Okay, church," he said, looking out over the crowd, "we have one final question to ask of you as witnesses to this joining. This is always the part of the ceremony that worries me most." He smiled at the chuckles that arose from the pews. "Before I free these two birds, I must ask, is there anyone in this church that sees why these two souls should not be joined together? If so, please speak now, or forever hold your peace."

Heads swiveled as everyone waited for someone to speak up. The church was quiet for several long moments. I glanced over at Todd, who was sweating profusely. He reached into his pocket for a handkerchief to mop up the sweat on his face. As he pulled the handkerchief out, a small piece of paper fluttered to the ground and landed by his foot.

"Are you okay?" the pastor asked him.

"What's that?" Chloe asked at the same time, using her free hand to point at the bit of paper.

Releasing Chloe's other hand, Todd knelt down, picked up the paper, and opened it.

# CHAPTER 44

**"It's nothing," Todd** said quickly, tucking the note back into his pocket. Chloe raised her eyebrow but didn't question him. I couldn't help but notice the turmoil on his face, but he took her hands again.

This is it. It looked like my brother was actually going through with it. The pastor moved to reopen his Bible, ready to read Todd and Chloe their vows.

Without warning, Todd's hand darted out to rest on the cover of the pastor's Bible.

"No," he said clearly and surprisingly calmly. The pastor stared at him uncomprehendingly.

"Todd," Chloe hissed. "What are you doing?"

"What are you doing, son?" the pastor repeated her question.

"What I should have done a long time ago," he replied. "No more lies," he added, loud enough this time that his words were heard throughout the sanctuary. As the guests murmured speculatively to one another, Todd turned to Chloe.

"I have something very important I need to say," he told her.

"Can't it wait?" she pleaded.

"No. It can't."

"Church," the pastor addressed the room, "before we proceed with the exchanging of the vows, the groom would like to say a few words."

"Todd, what are you doing?" asked Chloe again. He didn't answer, stepping a few feet to the right to remove the microphone from the wooden podium. As he loudly cleared his throat, a hush came over the room.

"Good afternoon, everyone. My name is Todd Banks, and I have been living a lie most of my life." The bridal party stood silently frozen as he addressed the crowd. "Up until quite recently, I thought my life looked pretty good. I even thought I was happy. Now I can see I was lying to myself, letting others direct me while pretending I was in control. I neither believed in God nor trusted Him to direct my path. Instead, I put my faith in myself and others. I did what I wanted, or so I believed."

Pausing, the room was still enough to hear a pin drop as everyone waited for his next words.

"Somehow, I convinced myself I wanted what other people wanted for me. But over the past six months, God has shown me the truth. I now know God is not only real, but very involved in my life. Though I questioned Him, He has answered my prayers repeatedly and sometimes very specifically. I even prayed for a sign from God this morning, giving Him a mere thirty minutes to give me concrete proof He was real. And He did, in a really powerful way."

He paced the few steps between the bridal party and the wooden podium. "What I'm trying to say is I'm tired of living for everyone else. I'm tired of pretending to be happy when I'm sad. I'm tired of leaving behind my dreams and trying to please other people, even those who don't give a damn about me. And I'm not going to do it any longer."

I grinned. Mr. Khakis had grown some balls.

"Instead, I'm going to let God lead. Because today, I gave my life to Jesus and I vowed to trust Him completely."

Shouts of "Amen!" broke out across the room. Interesting, I thought. *Looks like I haven't been the only one talking to God lately.*

Thinking he was finished, the pastor stepped forward, extending his hand for the mic. But Todd kept going.

"God has shown me that trusting Him means making choices, sometimes choices that are right, but not necessarily pleasing to everyone else." He glanced over at me, meeting my eyes briefly. "Fifteen months ago, I met a woman that changed the entire course of my life. This woman is truly the yin to my yang. And up until just a few hours ago, I thought I had lost her forever."

Chloe stared at him, hurt all over her face. Todd put down the mic and came towards her.

"I'm sorry, Chloe," he said softly. "You are an amazing woman, and you deserve the very best. You deserve someone who loves you wholeheartedly, without any reserve. I am sorry, but I am not that man. I cannot marry you. I'm in love with someone else, someone I cannot live without. I'm so, so sorry it took me until this moment to realize it."

I let out a breath I hadn't realized I'd been holding. "Finally," I said. Todd turned to me and nodded. Loving someone else was big, unexpected news, but it sounded like he was finally being honest with himself. I gave him a quick smile in return.

Ignoring the whispers circulating around the room, Todd descended the steps and headed back down the aisle. Before he could make it far, Chloe's father leaped out of his seat and lunged at him.

"You no-good bastard!" he shouted. Only the bridal party had been able to hear the end of Todd's confession, but it was obvious there was not going to be a wedding.

It looked like things were about to get out of control. I dashed from my post and jumped between Chloe's father and Todd. Grabbing him by the back of his jacket, I pushed him back and revealed my nine millimeter.

"Stay back!" I warned him. Todd shot me a grateful look, then ran for the exit with a giant grin on his face.

Nicole rushed up behind me. Before I could speak, my newfound family also approached. Surrounding us, they escorted us both away from the crowd.

"What the hell is going on?" Nicole asked me.

"I'll fill you in later," I promised. As we parted the double doors of the church, I spotted Todd getting into his car with a woman I had never seen before. I smiled. *Good for him.*

Just then, I felt my phone vibrate. Pulling it from the pocket of my tux, I glanced down at the screen. The name that appeared there stopped me in my tracks.

Sanchez was calling. It was time to hear the truth.

# New to the Secrets series?

*Enjoy all three books in the trilogy:*

## Secrets End
When criminal attorney Todd Banks uncovers a secret from his past, he finds himself questioning everything and everyone he knows. As he struggles to disentangle himself from an ever-expanding web of lies and betrayal, Todd discovers just how much his past has dictated his present.

## Secrets Begin
Growing up on the tough streets of Boston, where poverty and crime are the norm, and the only way out is in a body bag, prison or a miracle, fourteen-year-old Khalil Gilliam's life is turned upside down when a family secret is revealed.

Years later, he meets Todd Banks, a successful Boston attorney who reveals the truth about the secret buried years ago.

## Secrets Enemy
With their family secrets already exposed, Todd and Khalil believe they are finally in the clear... until Khalil learns the lies he and Todd uncovered go deeper than either of them ever believed.

As they strive to reveal the truth once and for all, they discover just how deeply the lies and deceit have infiltrated their inner circle. Not everyone who smiles at you is happy to see you.

*Read on for an excerpt from Secrets Enemy...*

# SECRETS ENEMY

## Book 3 of the SECRETS Trilogy

# PROLOGUE

**With my knees tucked up** in front of me, I peered out the crack outlining the door of Mom's antique armoire. I grinned to myself at my amazing hide-and-seek hiding spot. My brothers were both too big to fit inside the armoire. They'd never think to look for me here.

From my hideaway, I watched Mom preparing dinner in the kitchen. Down the hall, Dad was in his office, "getting ready for a court proceeding," whatever that meant.

The doorbell rang. "Honey," Mom leaned back and looked down the hallway, shouting towards Dad's office. "Can you answer the door?"

"Are you expecting guests?" he rang out, apparently bothered by the interruption.

"No," she shot back, "but you know my brother Martin always shows up when I make pot roast."

"Whatever happened to calling first?" Dad uttered in a bothered tone. "Damn freeloader."

From inside the armoire, I saw Mom frown. She quickly exited the kitchen, bumping the ancient piece of furniture with me inside as she passed by. She paused outside Dad's office door. "You know we are all he has since Mom and Dad passed a few years ago," she reminded him gently. "Take it easy on him, okay?"

Dad appeared in the doorway, taking Mom's hand. "Okay," he smiled. He leaned in to kiss her, and she smiled in response. Mom was one of the only people I'd ever seen break through Dad's defenses. Maybe it was because she was a psychiatrist, or maybe it was the way she looked at him that softened him up. Either way, it worked every time.

From my hiding spot, I heard my brothers approaching.

"Where could he be?" said Jason. "He has to be here somewhere." At just twelve years old and already nearly six feet tall, Jason was the best middle school athlete in the county. He excelled in both track and basketball.

"Yeah, but where?" voiced David, our oldest brother.

Without Jason's athletic gifts, David had made a name for himself as the neighborhood tyrant.

I froze as their footsteps crossed through the living room and approached my hiding spot. Holding my breath to keep from making a noise, I heard them rustling around, searching for me. I could also hear muffled voices coming from the front door.

Suddenly, I heard a thud in the entryway, and a loud scream rang out. Jason and David's movements stopped, then they quickly left the room. I heard them scream, too, followed by three more thuds. *What was happening?*

I peeked through the crack around the armoire door again, craning my neck to see into the living room. To my horror, I saw two very large men dressed in all black, wearing matching Batman masks. One of them had a gun, and it was pointed at Dad, who was tied up in a chair with blood running down the side of his face. My stomach knotted, and I shoved the back of my hand against my mouth to keep from screaming, too. *Who were they, and what did they want?*

"Let my wife and kids go," Dad pleaded. "They have nothing to do with this," he cried. He was staring down at the floor desperately. I followed his gaze. By the edge of the doorway, I could see three pairs of feet: Mom's, David's, and Jason's. Were they okay? They weren't moving or making any noise. *Surely Dad will get us all out of this,* I told myself confidently. But fear twisted my gut just the same.

"Get the tape to shut this fool up," one of the men motioned to his partner.

"I got the tape, boss," the other one said excitedly.

"Muzzle this loudmouth before I end him."

"No problem, boss." Pulling back, he punched Dad in the jaw with a straight right. Dad's head jerked with the blow, then sagged to the side. I gasped but managed to hide the noise with my hand.

"What the hell are you doing?"

"You told me to shut him up, boss."

"I meant with the tape, you idiot."

"Oh," he laughed. "Sorry, boss." He quickly tore off a piece of tape and slapped it across Dad's mouth.

How was Dad going to help now? Swallowing hard, I did the only thing I could think of. Mom had taught me God was there to help those who couldn't help themselves, and that was us right now. "Dear God, please save my family from these bad men, and hurry," I whispered quickly. "Amen."

"Now, before I end your worthless life, you piece-of-crap attorney," the boss man said to Dad coldly, "I want you to see what happens to people who mess with me." Reaching down, he yanked Mom to her feet. She whimpered as he maneuvered her to stand in front of Dad. From inside the armoire, I could see them standing in the living room doorway. The big man was holding Mom by her hair, and there were tears on her face. "Hand me one of those pillows," he demanded his sidekick, waving his gun at the couch.

"Here you go, boss."

"Say goodbye to your family," the man leered at Dad. He placed the pillow against Mom's face and, without warning, pulled the trigger. Her body collapsed, sagging to the floor.

My mind reeled. *This wasn't happening*. I squeezed my eyes closed, trying to shut it all out.

"Hey boss, can I get a piece of the action?"

The boss man nodded. "Sure, why not?"

My eyes popped back open as the sidekick grabbed David off the floor. Unlike Mom, David remained silent as he was pulled to his feet. Brandishing a sharp, silver knife, the sidekick grinned widely. Then he reached around and slit David's throat, dropping him to the floor as his body collapsed. A river of blood overflowed, quickly pooling on the living room floor. I tried not to, but I could smell the iron tang. I could also taste the salt of my own tears, silently pouring down my face.

James, still on the floor, twisted violently when David's body hit the ground next to him. Without another word, the boss aimed his gun at James and pulled the trigger.

"Any last words, mister hot shot attorney?" He ripped the tape off Dad's mouth.

"You will burn in hell for this."

"Doubtful." He raised his gun once more, aiming for the center of Dad's forehead, and pulled the trigger one final time. Dad's body jerked, then went limp.

"That's it, then. Let's get out of here, boss."

"No," the head henchman replied. "We can't leave yet." He plopped down on the chaise lounge, perusing the family photos on the end table. "The job is not done," he added.

"What are you talking about?" The sidekick looked ready to panic. "The police will be here any minute."

"This picture," he slammed his fist down on the table, then pointed. "What do you see?"

"It's the family we just killed. So what?"

"Look at the picture again, you idiot. There are five people in this picture. How many bodies do you see in this room?"

"Oh no. We missed one. Where is the other boy?"

# Acknowledgements

To the *greatest* influence in my life, GOD.

A special thanks to those who encouraged, inspired and or provided input during the time it took me to write this book: Mom, my daughter Ryan, Leslie, Brittany, Erin L., Jen C, Pamela, Brenda, Jeffrey, Stephen, Kim S., Malik, Angee C., Christina, Miranda, Adrienne, Kenny, Billy and Brandon.

CPSIA information can be obtained
at www.ICGtesting.com
Printed in the USA
LVHW040932250122
709311LV00005B/249